Dear Diary,

I may be thousands of miles away in Alaska, but the phone lines from Seattle are burning up with news of Forrester Square. According to Hannah and Alexandra, our little day care is still a hotbed of romance.

I wish I could have seen Alana Fletcher's face when she found herself "purchased" at the benefit auction by the day care's part-time carpenter, Sean Everett. Her son, Corey, set the whole thing up, with a little help from Hannah and Alexandra, of course.

Hannah says it looks as if one date could be turning into a hot and steamy romance—if only Alana will let it happen.

I don't know how she can resist. Sean is every woman's dream—handsome, sexy, good-humored. The kids at the day care love it when he's around. And if anyone deserves someone like Sean, it's Alana. She works so hard at being a good mom to Corey and a good vet to all her four-legged patients.

Well, Hannah and Alexandra have faith that Sean will eventually win her over. I sure hope so. But Alana's ex did a real number on her. Since the divorce, she's had her life perfectly laid out and doesn't want anything— or anyone—to change her plans.

I wonder how long it'll take her to realize that, try as you might, you just can't plan love.

Till tomorrow,

Katherine

DEBBI RAWLINS

currently lives in Las Vegas, Nevada. A native of Hawaii, she married on Maui and has since lived in Cincinnati, Chicago, Tulsa, Houston, Detroit and Durham, North Carolina, during the past twenty years. Debbi writes for Harlequin Temptation, Harlequin Blaze, Harlequin American Romance and Harlequin Duets. Her Las Vegas home has become a retreat for writers from both coasts, and her guest rooms are rarely empty. In fact, one friend visited with her cats three years ago and hasn't left yet!

Forrester Square

LEGACIES . LIES . LOVE .

DEBBI RAWLINS
BEST-LAID PLANS

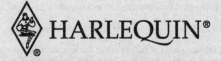

HARLEQUIN®

TORONTO • NEW YORK • LONDON
AMSTERDAM • PARIS • SYDNEY • HAMBURG
STOCKHOLM • ATHENS • TOKYO • MILAN • MADRID
PRAGUE • WARSAW • BUDAPEST • AUCKLAND

HARLEQUIN BOOKS
225 Duncan Mill Road, Don Mills,
Ontario, Canada M3B 3K9

ISBN 0-373-61278-8

BEST-LAID PLANS

Debbi Rawlins is acknowledged as the author of this work.

Copyright © 2003 by Harlequin Books S.A.

Visit us at www.eHarlequin.com

Printed in U.S.A.

Dear Reader,

Welcome to Forrester Square, where Alana Fletcher and Sean Everett find each other, thanks to a little help from Alana's precocious son, Corey.

Over the past few years I've really grown to like writing about kids. During my earlier books, the idea frankly scared me. Having no children of my own, I'd always worried that I had the kids in my books saying or doing things that weren't age appropriate. But then I acquired stepgrandchildren, ranging in ages from five to ten, and quickly found out that just about anything was likely to leave their mouths. And I do mean anything. Sheesh, did I worry for nothing!

That Corey Fletcher would decide his mother needed a husband and then go about finding one is hardly a stretch. I only wish I'd had such an advocate during my single years. Hope you enjoy his quest.

Best,

Debbi Rawlins

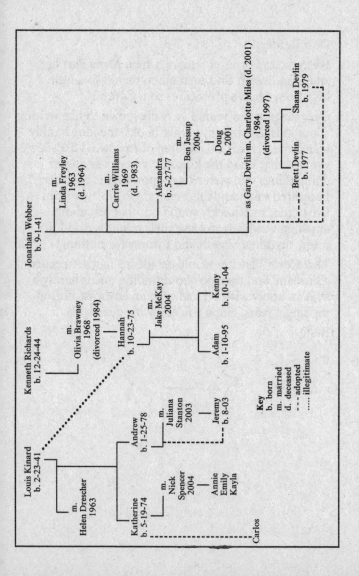

Louis Kinard
b. 2-23-41
m.
Helen Drescher
1963

Katherine
b. 5-19-74
m.
Nick Spencer
2004
Annie
Emily
Kayla

Andrew
b. 1-25-78
m.
Juliana Stanton
2003
Jeremy
b. 8-03

Carlos

Kenneth Richards
b. 12-24-44
m.
Olivia Brawney
1968
(divorced 1984)

Hannah
b. 10-23-75
m.
Jake McKay
2004
Adam
b. 1-10-95
Kenny
b. 10-1-04

Jonathan Webber
b. 9-1-41
m.
Linda Freyley
1963
(d. 1964)

m.
Carrie Williams
1969
(d. 1983)
Alexandra
b. 5-27-77
m.
Ben Jessup
2004
Doug
b. 2001

as Gary Devlin m. Charlotte Miles (d. 2001)
1984
(divorced 1997)

Brett Devlin
b. 1977
Shana Devlin
b. 1979

Key
b. born
m. married
d. deceased
- - - adopted
...... illegitimate

CHAPTER ONE

"DO YOU HAVE A WIFE?"

Sean Everett lowered his hammer and squinted down into a pair of earnest blue eyes. Using the back of his sleeve, he wiped the sweat off his forehead. Warm for Seattle, especially this early in the morning.

"Did you hear me, mister? I wanna know if you have a wife."

Working around Forrester Square Day Care on and off for the past year, Sean had been asked a number of odd questions, but this one took the cake. He tried not to laugh. "Why?"

The little blond boy shrugged. He looked to be about five or six, new to the day care probably. Sean didn't recognize him. "Just because."

"No reason at all, huh?"

The kid stuck his hands into his jeans' pockets and shrugged again, this time avoiding Sean's eyes.

Sean tried not to smile. "Do you?"

"Huh?"

"Have a wife?"

The boy made a face. "I'm just a kid."

"Ah." Sean stifled a yawn. Getting up at four-thirty every morning for the past week was getting to him. "Okay. I don't have a wife."

The boy broke out into a toothy grin. "Perfect."

Sean had a bad feeling about this. "Why?"

"Corey!"

They both turned toward the voice. One of the day care aides stood in the doorway and vigorously motioned for the boy.

"Uh-oh. I'm late again." He started to run in her direction, stopped and said, "I'll see you later, dude."

Sean laughed as he watched the boy scamper off. God only knew what the little guy was up to. Kids rarely made sense. Hell, most adults didn't, either. He switched the hammer to his other hand and dragged his damp palm down the front of his jeans before gripping the handle again.

Before he could take a swing, he saw one of the day care owners crossing the playground and headed toward him. He discarded the hammer, picked up his thermos and unscrewed the top while he waited for her to approach. "Morning, Sean."

Alexandra Webber handed him a glazed doughnut wrapped in a napkin.

"You're an angel." His stomach rumbled. He didn't hesitate to take a big bite.

"Not exactly. I came out here to harass you." She made an apologetic face as her gaze darted toward the half-completed stage. "Please tell me it'll be finished by next weekend."

Okay, so he'd start getting up at three-thirty. "Have I ever let you down?"

She smiled. "Don't mind me. I'm nervous about the auction."

"I know." Sean patted her arm. She reminded him of his older sister, spirited and to the point. Even the short red hair was similar.

He missed Maureen. And her brood. Although he'd visited them last month when she gave birth to his youngest nephew, there was no telling when he'd get to see them again.

Maureen's husband was air force. A captain, just like their dad had been, and that meant an unpredictable future. With only two weeks' notice, they could be packed up and shipped off to Greenland or some other obscure corner of the earth.

Been there, done that. Sean liked Seattle just fine. After living here only three years, the city was already starting to feel like home.

"I'm probably driving everyone crazy with all my worrying." Alexandra ran a finger over the rough edge of the first step. "Hannah has threatened to muzzle me. It's just lucky Katherine's still in Alaska."

Hannah and Katherine were the other two owners of the day care, and Sean enjoyed working for both of them. "Will she be back for the auction?"

"I doubt it." Alexandra's green eyes sparkled with laughter. "She said she'd only be gone a week, but I have a feeling she may be otherwise occupied."

"That guy Nick?" Sean had seen him around a few times. Who'd have figured he was Katherine's type?

She nodded. "He's a bush pilot. So he's showing her the Alaska sights."

"Hmm, never used that line before."

Alexandra laughed. "Me, neither."

He set down the thermos and then touched the same spot on the step Alexandra had examined. "All this is going to be nice and smooth by the weekend. Promise."

"I know, Sean, and I appreciate the great job you're doing. Believe me, I've noticed how early you start and how late you stay. Not to mention keeping up with your own workload. And you're not charging us nearly enough." She winced. "Not that we're in a position to argue."

"Hey, you asked for a quote and I gave it to you. A deal is a deal." He picked up the hammer again, anxious to end the conversation and get back to work.

No way would he charge the women a penny for his labor. They'd argue when he turned down the money, but he could be as stubborn as a jackass when he had a mind to be. The financial backer of the day care, a man called Jordan Edwards, had died suddenly, and his heirs were calling in the loan. The three partners, Katherine, Hannah and Alexandra, had agreed to hold a benefit auction to pay off the loan. If they didn't raise enough money, they'd end up closing shop. This would be his contribution.

Alexandra smiled when he took a swing at a nail. "Okay, I get the hint. I'll get out of your hair, but you'd better keep an eye on the time. I'm sure you have another job to get to soon, and traffic is horrible this morning."

"Yes, ma'am." He glanced at his watch. Seventwenty. He had half an hour to get over to old man

Cooper's hardware store, where he was adding a storage shed in the back.

"Stop by the office if you want a refill for your thermos," Alexandra said as she headed back toward the three-story sandstone building that housed the day care.

Sean looked up and saw the blond kid he'd been talking to earlier. The boy stood in the doorway, staring out at them. "Alexandra, wait."

She stopped.

"Who's the new kid?" He gestured with his chin.

She glanced over her shoulder and then gave him a teasing grin. "Corey Fletcher. He's been coming here for about a month. I take it he's been sizing you up, too."

"What do you mean?"

"Hannah saw him checking out the dads picking up their kids. He asked some of them if they were married." Her smile widened. "So, did you make the final cut?"

"Very funny." He looked at his watch again.

"His mother is a veterinarian, divorced, and Corey's the only child. Sounds like he might be trying to match-make."

Sean shook his head. He'd bet Corey's mother would be real happy to hear that.

"Don't forget to stop by the office," Alexandra said, and took off again.

He pushed his stubborn hair off his forehead. He had to either get a haircut really soon or find a way to tie it back. Although there wasn't much he could do about the top. The damn thing had been falling in his eyes since he was a kid.

Using the level, he made sure the step he was about to nail was flat and even. He didn't have much time left this morning if he wanted to take Alexandra up on that refill offer.

He stood back and surveyed today's progress. No getting around it. He'd have to work late tonight. After quitting at the hardware store, he'd swing by his apartment and pick up a couple of floodlights. No way would he let Alexandra, Hannah and Katherine down.

"DO YOU THINK THIS IS gonna be enough?" Corey asked, and his friend made a sound of disgust. "Well, how much do you think it'll cost?"

"I dunno." Ritchie snorted. "Why are you asking me, anyway?"

"Duh, who else am I gonna ask? My mom?"

Alana Fletcher stood outside the kitchen door, her arms full of a frisky chocolate Lab puppy, smiling as she listened to her son chatting with his new friend from down the street. Corey hadn't adjusted easily to the move from Olympia to Seattle. He missed his friends and he especially missed his father. Even though his father didn't give a damn about him.

At the thought of her ex-husband, Alana's smile faded. Although she'd already come to terms with his rejection and immaturity, she hated that he ignored Corey. Brad had lived only four miles away from them, yet thought nothing of seeing his son only once every two months.

Alana had gotten tired of watching the hope in her little boy's eyes turn to disappointment every weekend that Brad didn't show up. As much as she'd hated leaving her thriving vet practice, she saw no alternative but to move. Far enough away that she didn't have to make excuses for her selfish, irresponsible ex. And she didn't have to watch the anguish on Corey's face.

"I bet your mom gets mad," Ritchie said, snagging Alana's attention.

"No, she won't." Corey sounded firm.

"Bet she does."

"I'll bet you my new bike she doesn't."

Alana nearly choked. She was about to interrupt before the wager was cemented, but the Lab puppy took care of the matter for her. He wiggled out of her arms, jumped to the floor and scampered toward the boys' voices.

Ritchie gasped. "Where did he come from?"

Alana entered the kitchen just as Corey looked up with wide eyes. His gaze went to the piggy bank he'd cracked open, and then to the neatly stacked coins beside it, and finally back to Alana.

"Hi, Mom. You're home early. Is this a new patient?" He avoided her gaze and bent to pick up the puppy. "My mom's a doctor, you know," he told Ritchie.

Alana smiled wryly. The little con artist was trying to distract her from asking the obvious. "A veterinarian."

"That's an animal doctor."

Ritchie made a face. "I know what veterinarian

means. We take our cat to a vet once a year. Except he's fat and old and smells funny.''

From Ritchie's description, Alana knew exactly to which of her peers the little boy referred. ''What's this out for?'' she asked, using her chin to indicate the piggy bank as she reached for the squirming puppy.

Corey gave up the dog but avoided her gaze. ''I was just counting how much money I've saved.''

''Why?''

Her son looked at Ritchie, whose mouth lifted in a wide grin. After sliding him a warning look, Corey said, ''I just wanna know.''

''Really?'' Alana raised a teasing brow. ''You have a date I don't know about?''

Ritchie shrieked with laughter.

Corey's cheeks ripened to the color of strawberries. ''That's gross, Mom.''

''But you sort of are saving for a date,'' Ritchie chimed in, before dissolving into a giggling fit.

''Am not.'' Corey gave his friend a murderous glare.

''Yeah, but—''

Corey clamped his hand over Ritchie's mouth, and when the boy jerked in anger, Alana stepped forward.

''Hey, you two.'' Gently she tugged at the sleeve of Corey's red and white striped rugby shirt. ''What's the problem?''

''Nothing,'' Corey mumbled.

Ritchie shrugged. ''We're just playing.''

She let go of her son. ''Then how about playing a little nicer?''

"I gotta go home, anyway." Ritchie darted Corey a tentative look. "See you tomorrow."

Corey nodded and watched his friend leave through the kitchen door before he asked, "Mom, do you miss Dad?"

Alana's heart thudded as she looked into her son's anxious blue eyes. "Sometimes," she said slowly, "as I'm sure you do."

He nodded, the same sad look on his face as the day they'd left Olympia.

The urge to retreat to her backyard clinic and avoid the conversation altogether nearly made her turn away. But that would reduce her to Brad's level, and Corey didn't need or deserve another aloof parent.

Besides, this was her job. She couldn't expect the hugs and smiles and not participate in the other stuff that went with being a parent. Anyway, this was good. Really. Corey should feel free to discuss his dad and his feelings about their recent move, about their new home. Truly, this was good.

She swallowed hard. "Do you miss your old school and friends?"

He shrugged. "Sometimes."

"We're not that far, and you know we'll be visiting a lot. And of course your daddy will come here to see you."

His eyes lit up. "When?"

"I'll have to talk with him. We haven't figured out a weekend that works yet." She adjusted the wriggling puppy in her arms but looked up in time to see the hope fade from her son's face. "But I'm planning on calling him and we'll settle on a weekend, okay?"

"When?"

"Well, honey, that's what we have to discuss. You know your father is busy even on the—"

"No, I mean when are you calling him?"

She hesitated. But there was only one answer that would do. "Tonight." She ruffled his hair, already dreading the phone call she'd promised to make. "Now, how about washing up for dinner?"

"Can I help you walk the dogs first?"

"We have only two overnighters and Cindy is walking them right now."

"Can I feed them then?"

Alana knew her assistant would take care of that, too. "Okay, go help Cindy, but when you're done you wash up, and no argument, okay?"

He nodded but made no attempt to go. "Mom?"

God, but she hated that tone. Whatever came next would make her feel guilty. She forced a smile. "Yes?"

"Don't you get lonely?"

She laughed softly. "How can I? I've got you and Saffron. And all the animals at the clinic…"

"That's not the same. You don't have any friends."

"Of course I do. There's Mrs. Lemon from the library, and my assistant, Cindy, and now Hannah and all the others at the day care—" She stopped when he started shaking his head. "What's wrong?"

"That's not the same either."

She narrowed her gaze. "Young man, are you trying to avoid your bath?"

His eyes widened. "No, Mom, honest." He made a cross over his heart. "I just worry about you."

Alana caught her lower lip between her teeth. He was only six years old. Too young to worry, especially about his mother. She crouched down beside him and hugged him to her. "Honey, there's nothing to worry about. I love Seattle, our new house, and having the clinic in our own backyard. Don't you?"

"Yeah."

"I've never worked so close to home before. Isn't it nice?"

"Yeah, but—" He shrugged.

"But what?" She playfully poked under his arm, getting a giggle out of him. "Tell me."

He looked at her, serious again. "Don't you want a boyfriend?"

She coughed. "A what?"

Embarrassment flooded his face. "You know…" He shrugged. "Someone to play with. Hannah said that—"

It must have been the angry heat that crawled up her neck and filled her face that stopped him.

"Go on. What did she say?"

"Nothing, Mom."

"Corey."

"I'm hungry." He squirmed out of her arms. "I think I'll go get washed up now."

She rose, for a moment seriously considering making him stay put until he spilled the gossip about her.

She sighed, feeling silly. The women at the day care center weren't the type to gossip.

He grabbed the coins he'd stacked on the table, dropped some of them back into his piggy bank, and stuffed the rest into his pockets. "Mom, how can I get more allowance?"

"If you need anything—"

He shook his head. "This is different. Can I do extra chores or something?"

"How much do you need?" she asked, shamelessly fishing, her curiosity piqued.

His face scrunched up. "I'm not sure."

And then it dawned on her. Brad's birthday was coming up in a couple of weeks. Corey probably wanted to buy a present for his father.

Childishly, the idea irked the hell out of her that Corey wanted to work extra just to buy his selfish, insensitive father a gift. But the adult in her understood that Corey loved his father, warts and all. He'd want to please the man, try and garner his attention. Natural behavior. Still, it broke her heart.

"Well, whatever you need, I'm sure we can work it out," she said, trying hard not to think about the day Brad told her she wasn't fun anymore, then packed his bags and hopped into Sheila Sutton's red convertible.

"Cool." He gave her a big toothy grin that melted her heart and chased away the ugly memories.

She gestured toward the back door. "Okay, now go help Cindy with the dogs and then straight to the bathroom."

Halfway there he stopped. "Hey, Mom, we're going to the auction next weekend, aren't we?"

"I hadn't planned on it."

"But, Mom..." he drawled out the word. "We have to go."

"Why?"

"Everyone else is going."

She rubbed the back of her neck. A headache had seized the base of her skull. Buying the modest three-bedroom house and moving her practice had left them with very little disposable cash. Certainly not enough to be spending at auctions. "Honey, I've already donated a year of my services."

He wrinkled his nose. "So?"

She shook her head at herself. Corey wasn't concerned about their finances, or how much money the day care raised. "You want to go because your friends are going?"

He nodded vigorously. "Okay, sport." She tossed him the baseball cap he'd left on the table. "We'll go for a little while."

What the heck. What else did she have to do on a Friday night, besides be dragged to St. Michael's for a game of bingo with Ida and Miriam?

CHAPTER TWO

"HEY, MISTER, WAIT UP!"

Sean heard the youthful voice but he didn't turn around. The playground swarmed with people, most of whom he didn't know. Couldn't be him the kid was calling.

"Hey."

A tug on his shirt stopped him and he finally turned around. It was the blond kid from last week. Corey—or maybe it was Cody.

"Hey yourself." He tugged down the bill of the boy's Mariner's baseball hat. "What's going on?"

The kid pushed the cap back up and eyed him with annoyance. "You're going in the wrong direction."

Sean frowned. "I am? Where am I supposed to be going?"

"The auction is starting any second."

He stared into the boy's flushed face. Mustard smeared the corner of his mouth, but his eyes shone with excitement. He glanced over his shoulder, took a thorough look around, and then faced Sean again with a relieved expression.

Sean gazed over his head to see who he might be scouting out, but it was impossible to tell with so many people crowding toward the stage. He met the boy's anxious eyes. "It's Corey, right?"

The boy nodded. "We have to hurry."

"That's the thing, Corey. I have no idea what you're talking about."

"The auction is about to start."

"Yup, it is." Sean rubbed his jaw. He probably should have shaved again. "Do you want me to watch it with you? Is that it?"

"Yeah, but first…" He pulled out a bunch of crumpled bills from his pocket, then a small plastic bag full of loose change. He tried to hand both to Sean. "Here."

Sean reared back his head. "What?"

"This is to buy my mom."

"To what?" Obviously he'd heard wrong.

"You know…to…" He wrinkled his nose. "What's that word called?"

"Look, aren't you here with anyone? They're probably looking for you."

Corey sighed with disgust. "I know, so hurry up and take this. You gotta buy my mom."

"Look, kiddo, I don't know who your mom is, and I doubt she'd be happy about you—"

"Right there." Corey pointed toward the day care center, and then hid behind Sean. "But I don't want her to see me."

In spite of himself, Sean peered across the playground into the crowd. Most everyone was paired up. Except two women, one standing alone and the other talking to a couple with their fidgeting toddler.

"Is she blond like you?" Sean asked.

"Nope."

"Brunette?" Sean's gaze lingered on the taller woman, whose hair was pulled back in some kind of twist.

"Huh?" Corey's brow wrinkled in confusion.

"Dark hair?"

"Yeah. Do you see her?" He poked his head out.

"Does she have on a long flowery skirt and white blouse?"

"I think so. Her shirt's white, anyway. She wears skirts a lot. But sometimes jeans." He ducked again. "Son of a B, I think she saw me."

Sean choked back a laugh. Somehow he didn't think the woman he assumed was Corey's mother would approve of that kind of language. She looked a little old-fashioned with her long flowing skirt and filmy white blouse, especially with her hair pulled back. Not in a severe style, though. Lots of wispy flyaway curls gave her a soft look.

He turned his attention to Corey. "Does she know about this?"

"About what?" The innocent look was a sham.

Sean narrowed his gaze impatiently.

Corey gave a noncommittal shrug. "My mom donated her services. She told me that herself."

He bit back a laugh. "Donated her services?"

The little boy nodded solemnly. "That's what she said."

Sean couldn't wait to hear this explanation. "But I didn't see her name on the schedule."

"Huh?"

"The list of items up for bid."

Corey's frown deepened, his serious blue eyes looking way too old for someone his age.

"Never mind." Sighing, Sean shoved his hair off his forehead and studied the earnestness on the boy's face. He probably didn't even know what the word *bid* meant. "Why do you want me to bid on her?"

"Because she's lonely. She doesn't have any friends."

The innocent explanation took him aback. He knew all too well what it felt like to be the new kid on the base, to have to worm your way into cliques or pretend you didn't care that no one made an attempt to befriend you. "Where's your father?" he finally asked.

Corey's face clouded. "He lives in Olympia." Corey shrugged, as if it didn't matter. "We don't get to see him much."

"Ah." Sean remembered now. Alexandra had said something about the woman being divorced or separated. Tough break for the kid. Sean sighed. He didn't want to disappoint the poor little guy, but... "Look, let's play it by ear."

"Play what?"

"We'll just see how things go."

"But you will buy her, right?" Corey's anxious voice made Sean want to get in his pickup truck and head up the coast for parts unknown.

Someone on the stage started messing with the loudspeaker. The awful screeching noise coming from the microphone was a perfect distraction.

The auction is about to start," Sean said, and nodded his head toward Corey's mother. "Your mom's looking for you."

"Son of a B." Corey angled his head to see. "I gotta go. Here." He stuffed the crumpled bills and some change into Sean's hand, spilling some of it on the ground, then took off before Sean got out a single word.

"HAVE YOU SEEN COREY?"

Hannah shook her head with an apologetic shrug as she passed Alana and hurried toward the stage, toting a poster board with pink lettering.

Of course he was safe. Alana got up on tiptoes to survey the swelling crowd. The playground of Forrester Square day care was packed with supporters and eager bidders studying the auction items. Most of them were parents, like herself, who didn't want the center to close. She needn't worry. But then again...

"Alexandra," she called out to one of Hannah's partners. "Have you seen Corey?"

Alexandra pointed toward the stage. Alana squinted, still not spotting her son. And then with a surge of relief she saw him, staring up at a tall, light-haired man in jeans. No one she recognized.

Granted, from this distance she couldn't make out the man's face, but she could see his smile. Wide and brilliantly white, it was hard to miss.

Starting toward them, she bobbed her head above the crowd to keep track of Corey in case he ran off again. He knew better than to leave her side without saying where he was going. Except the little bugger had been acting pretty strange all week, and that made her nervous.

She stuffed her chilly hands into her skirt pocket and found a loose breath mint. The taste of the hot dog and sauerkraut she'd just had for dinner lingered on her tongue, and after checking for lint, she gratefully popped the white disk into her mouth.

"I don't blame you. He's really something, isn't he?" Hannah came up from behind, minus the poster, and linked an arm through Alana's. "Have you tried the caramel apples? They're worth every pound added to my thighs."

"Who's really something?" As soon as the words left her mouth, Alana realized she'd been staring at the man talking with Corey. She blinked at Hannah, wondering whether a denial would make matters worse.

Hannah chuckled. "It's okay—we've all gawked at him. Especially when he works without his shirt. Sean built the stage for us."

Alana stiffened. As if she'd be ogling a man, especially one that young and good looking. Right. She needed a migraine more than she needed a man. "I was looking for my son."

"Uh-huh. Conveniently he's with Sean." Hannah grinned. "I'm just teasing. Don't get so uptight."

Something Corey had said last week came to mind. "Hannah, Corey made a remark that's bothered me. I think he might have overheard something you said."

Alana hesitated, not wanting to sound accusatory. "About me."

Hannah shrugged. "Like what?"

She cringed inwardly, wishing she hadn't brought up the subject. Not now, anyway. "Maybe you mentioned something about me needing to make friends," she said tactfully. "I'm not really sure."

The other woman shook her head, obviously a little hurt. "I haven't been gossiping about you, if that's what you mean."

Heat stung Alana's cheeks. "I didn't mean anything, Hannah. I'm sorry. It's just that—" Alana shook her head. "It's just me. Corey's been acting strange all week, and then we get here and he eats a hot dog and disappears before I finish paying for his popcorn."

An expression that looked almost like guilt flickered across Hannah's face. "All the kids have been excited over the auction. Nothing to worry about, I'm sure." Her gaze darted away. "Alexandra is calling me. I'll talk to you later."

Standing alone again, Alana sighed. It was entirely possible Corey had overheard a conversation between her and Hannah. Once they'd talked over a cup of coffee when Hannah had brought a stray gray tabby into the clinic. She'd discovered the kitten behind the day care center, and Alana had treated him for malnutrition and then found him a home.

Alana tried to recall what had been said. Nothing terribly specific came to mind, but it had been one of those dreary days that had Alana feeling a little melancholic, and she'd done something she rarely did. She'd openly talked about the divorce and how it had changed her life.

Oh, God, she hoped Corey hadn't heard any of it. He'd been playing in the backyard with two of the collies they were boarding. He could have come to the kitchen for some water and stood at the back door...

But he would have said something later, she was quite sure. He wasn't reticent about asking her questions. He had at least three dozen a day. Maybe he'd only heard part of what she'd said...apparently the part about her being lonely.

But she wasn't, really. Hannah thought she was, but Alana was quite content. Truly.

She chomped down hard on the breath mint and inadvertently bit the inside of her cheek, making her wince. Darn it. Anyway, Corey had no excuse for taking off like that. She wouldn't embarrass him here, but when they got home...

She narrowed her gaze at the stage. He had disappeared again. So had his friend. She glanced to the left and then to the right. He was in serious trouble now. Especially since she was pretty sure he'd seen her.

"Hey, Mom."

"Where have you been, young man?" she demanded, spinning toward Corey's voice.

"Just talking to Sean."

"And who is this person?"

"A friend."

"I figured out that much. But how do you know

him?'' She had the sudden and annoying realization that her interest went beyond her son's welfare.

Corey barely listened to her. His attention kept wandering toward the stage. ''Come on, Mom. The auction's gonna start. We need to find a seat up front.''

''Why?''

He grabbed her hand and dragged her through the crowd. She spotted his friend Sean not far from the back of the stage and was relieved that Corey didn't seem to be heading that way. She got a good look at the man though, and had to admit he was nothing to sneeze at.

Not exactly blond, his hair was more sun-streaked, as if he worked outdoors a lot. Which he did, according to Hannah. His arms were nicely muscled, too, not overly so, but a woman would certainly know when he had them around her waist.

''There, Mom.'' Corey jerked her hand, startling her, and making her realize she'd been staring. ''Hannah saved two seats for us.''

Hannah waved them toward her. She had reserved the end two seats in the first row. Alana truly wished she hadn't done that. People who actually planned on bidding should have the front row seats.

As soon as they got within hearing distance, Alana said, ''We'll just stand on the side.''

Hannah pointed. ''Sit.''

Alana laughed at the unexpected command. ''Where are you going to be?''

''On stage helping Alexandra. Promise me you'll stay right here.''

"But it's ridiculous to—"

Alana shook her head. Hannah had already moved away, and Corey had claimed one of the seats. She lowered herself down beside him and waited, along with everyone else, for Alexandra to get the microphone to work.

The crowd seemed patient. Most people knew the auction had been put together on a shoestring. Everyone interested in keeping the day care open had pulled together, donating time and services, begging and borrowing for this auction. Although Forrester Square had been operating less than a year, its stellar reputation had ensured a constant waiting list.

Within a couple of minutes, Alexandra had adjusted the microphone and began the program with a brief but heartfelt thank-you speech. Wasting no more time, she introduced a volunteer who had experience in livestock auctions back in Wyoming, where he'd raised cattle.

Floyd was a short round man with a flushed smiling face and a voice so loud and fast that the audience gave a collective start. It didn't seem to faze him, and the bidding began with rip-roaring laughter.

Alana relaxed in her seat, happy to see the excitement on Corey's face, to hear him laugh so hard at the auctioneer that tears filled his eyes. Maybe she wouldn't take away television for three days. After all, he'd never disappeared like that before. A good scolding would probably do.

The list of items and the final bids were quite impressive. One offering in particular caught Alana's attention—a makeover and fashion session donated by local celebrity model J. J. Jamison. Not that Alana could afford it, or needed it for her simple lifestyle, but it sounded fun and girlie and decadent. Of course, it went quickly for a phenomenal amount.

Half an hour into the bidding, Alana started to yawn. She checked her watch. How could it be only eight-forty? One glance at Corey told her they wouldn't be going anywhere soon. She didn't have the heart to tear him away.

She yawned again, then frowned when she thought she heard the auctioneer say her name. Of course that wasn't possible…

Corey tugged at her arm.

Several people turned to stare.

She blinked at her son. "What is it?"

"He wants you to go on the stage, Mom."

"Who?"

"That man." Corey pointed to the short rotund auctioneer. Behind him, Hannah stood smiling and motioned for Alana to get up. "Come on, Mom, hurry."

She shook her head. This didn't make sense. Sure, she'd offered veterinary services for a year, but none of the other donors had been called onto the stage.

Or had they? Maybe she'd been daydreaming…

"Mom…" Corey dragged out the word. "We can't wait all night."

Alexandra appeared beside her and drew her to her feet. "This won't take long," she said, smiling. "I promise."

"What won't take long?" Alana stumbled toward

the steps to the stage, trying to decide how much of a scene she was willing to make. Before taking the first step, she gently jerked out of her friend's hold. She swept a sidelong glance toward the audience. All eyes were on her.

She hated being the center of attention. Detested it. Her heart pounded, her palms grew damp, and she turned away from the stares. This reminded her of veterinary school, when she'd had to give an oral presentation to a group of first-year students. She'd stuttered and stammered and turned several shades of red and purple, even though she thoroughly knew the material.

"Alexandra," she whispered, while taking a step back. "I can't go up on that stage."

"It'll only be for about three minutes."

She gave a firm shake of her head. "It doesn't matter. There's no reason for me to—"

"Look, it's for Corey," Alexandra cut in. "He has a surprise for you."

Corey? She turned to meet his eyes. Anxious eyes. Full of hope and excitement. She knew he'd been up to something. Darn. Darn. Darn.

She swallowed hard, slowly took the steps up to the stage and made a point of looking above the audience members' heads. No eye contact and just maybe she'd make it through the next few minutes without embarrassing herself. Maybe.

The auctioneer approached, took her hand and led her to the center of the stage. Thankfully, Floyd made no comment about her sweaty palm, but only winked before turning to the audience and starting his rapid-fire spiel.

Even when she wasn't nervous, it had been difficult to understand him. Now she didn't have the faintest idea what he was saying. She knew only that the audience reacted with murmurs, quickly followed by laughter.

Mortified, she looked helplessly at Hannah, who seemed preoccupied with scouring the crowd. Corey had risen from his seat and he too bobbed and twisted as if looking for someone or something.

"Come on, now, folks," Floyd said in a normal voice. "Look at this young lady here. I'm surprised you single, red-blooded men out there aren't jumping to make the first bid."

Alana blinked, surprised at the gender qualification. "Anyone can bid on my services."

Someone from the audience howled with laughter, which was quickly followed by a chorus of hilarity.

"Well now, that's a fact, ma'am," Floyd said with a wink to the audience, which caused more laughter.

Alana didn't get it. What was so damn funny about a year of vet service? Surely most of these people understood how much that package was worth.

"Tell you what, folks…" Floyd pursed his lips, his bushy graying eyebrows drawing together. "Let's start the bidding at, say—"

"Twelve-sixty-seven."

The deep male voice came from beyond the last row of seats. Several people turned to look. Alana shaded her eyes from the glare of the lights strung over the stage. She still couldn't see a thing.

"Did I hear right?" Floyd narrowed his gaze as he also tried to locate the bidder. "You're bidding twelve hundred and sixty seven dollars?"

The audience let out a collective gasp.

"No, mister." Corey jumped out of his seat and ran to the foot of the stage. "He means twelve dollars and sixty-seven cents."

The people in the first few rows who could hear him erupted into laughter. Alana's cheeks flamed with humiliation. What did Corey have to do with this? What the hell was going on? She turned in search of Alexandra or Hannah...

"Make that one hundred dollars," the mysterious voice called out.

"Now we're talkin'." Floyd grinned, and started his speedy auctioneer routine.

A few seconds into his gibberish, someone else yelled, "A hundred and fifty."

Alana shuddered. That sounded an awful lot like Morgan Stern, the taxidermist who had a shop on the next block from her clinic. The guy didn't have a single living pet. Why would he bid on her services?

"Well, now, folks, glad to see that you're getting in the spirit of this here auction. Very important auction, I'll remind you. Do I hear two hundred?"

"Two hundred." The same voice that had started the bidding. But this time the person stepped forward, the light reflecting off the blond streaks in his hair.

It was Sean...Corey's friend.

Alana's breath caught. Not just because of the breadth of his shoulders, or the way his jeans hugged his long legs, or even because of the slow sexy smile that spread across his tanned face. But it was the way he looked at her, the intensity in his eyes, as if she were the only person there, as if they weren't being stared at by half the population of Seattle.

He stopped directly in front of the stage and repeated, "Two hundred."

Hannah appeared from nowhere, grabbed the microphone from Floyd, and said, "Sold. Sean Everett has just bought a date with Alana Fletcher's new friend."

CHAPTER THREE

"WE DON'T EXPECT YOU TO pay the two hundred," Hannah said to Sean quickly, glancing over her shoulder at Alana as she navigated the steps. "I hadn't expected Morgan to get in on the action. But I should've known."

Sean kept his gaze on Alana, the graceful way she lifted her long skirt to take another stair. She had slim ankles, a nice curve to her calves. He knew she was a vet, but she seemed so graceful, she looked more like the women who worked in those expensive fashion boutiques on Queen Anne Avenue.

"Sean?"

He blinked at Hannah.

"Are you listening?" Her sly grin made him straighten.

He loosened his shoulders. "I'll give you the two hundred tomorrow. I don't have my checkbook with me."

"No way." She gave a firm shake of her head. "Alexandra told me you wouldn't accept payment for building the stage. You've done enough for us."

"Look, we'll talk about it later, okay?" Sean murmured as Alana and Corey approached.

Or more accurately—as Corey dragged his mother toward them.

"Here she is, Sean." With a victorious grin, Corey jerked his mother's hand and she stumbled forward another step.

Alana's cheeks flamed an unnatural pink and she gave her son a stern look. "Corey, we have to go home now."

His eyes went wide with indignation. "But, Mom, you haven't met Sean yet."

Hannah laughed. "Cry uncle, Alana."

"*You,* I will speak with later." She gave the other woman a meaningful look and then her gaze flickered to Sean. "I'm sorry about all this."

He shrugged. "Why? It's for a good cause."

She opened her mouth to speak, but the auctioneer had gone on to announce that the next item was a year of Dr. Alana Fletcher's vet services. She sighed heavily and shook her head.

"What's wrong?" He thought he knew, but wanted to start up the conversation.

She made a motion toward the auctioneer, who'd begun taking bids on her donated services. "*That's* why I thought I was on stage."

"Ah." He smiled. "On the bright side, you were such a good sport, it sounds like everyone's bidding high on your donation."

"Swell."

"Look, let's step over here." The curious stares and chuckling from the audience were even starting to get to him. He guided the group a few steps back into the shadows, and Alana seemed to relax. Too bad he couldn't see her face more clearly.

"Look, I'm sorry about anything my son roped you into," she said. "I'll, uh—" She sighed. "I'll make good on the two hundred dollars so the center won't be out any money."

"No way." Sean shook his head. "A deal is a deal. Right, Corey?"

The sharp look she gave her son made Sean regret getting the poor little guy into more trouble.

Corey's expression fell. "But, Mom, you said I could use my allowance to buy whatever I wanted."

Surprise flared in her gaze, and then a sadness he couldn't interpret.

"He's been saving every penny for over a week," Hannah said.

"That's what the extra chores were for," Alana murmured, her love for her son so clear on her face, something funny stirred inside Sean.

"It's okay, Mom." He shrugged his narrow shoulders. "I know you're lonely. I didn't mind spending it to buy you a friend."

Immediately the affection was replaced with a murderous glare. "Corey, let's go." She took his arm and avoided Sean's gaze.

Sean laughed. He couldn't help it.

Hannah ran interference. She laid a hand on Alana's arm but addressed Corey. "Have you had any cotton candy yet?"

He shook his head, a grin lighting his face.

"Hannah, please…" Alana met the other woman's

eyes, but the wordless communication was lost on Sean.

He could sure guess, though. Alana was obviously embarrassed, and he couldn't blame her. If the situation had been reversed, he probably would've grounded the kid until he was twenty-one.

For a few seconds Sean considered being chivalrous and letting her slip away to lick her wounds. But damn it, now he was interested. Something about her called to him, almost as if he had known her for a long time, or maybe shared a past life with her. He didn't really believe in that sort of stuff, but now he understood how some people could.

Hell, if he didn't use this opportunity, he might never get to know her.

"What's it going to hurt?" Hannah asked, her voice soft and coaxing. "Just talk awhile. It sure would make you-know-who happy."

Alana looked grudgingly down into her son's earnest eyes.

"Besides, I'm starting to get a complex," Sean said, earning a small lift of her lips.

Hannah winked. "Corey and I will be back in ten or fifteen minutes."

Alana pressed her lips together. She looked as if she wanted to protest, but kept quiet.

After the other two were out of earshot, Sean said, "You have quite a kid there. Very enterprising."

"I'm really sorry—"

He put a silencing finger to her lips, surprising both

of them. She blinked and moved her head a little, enough to break contact.

He lowered his hand. "No more unnecessary apologies. Corey obviously loves you very much. I think it's great he cares enough to find you a friend."

She laughed softly, the sound so pleasant it warmed him down to his toes. "How diplomatic of you."

Sean smiled. "So, what night is good for you?"

Alana frowned. "For what?"

"Our date."

"Don't you understand?" Her hazel eyes narrowed. "I'm letting you off the hook."

"And if I don't want to be let off?"

She stared in stunned silence, and then she crossed her arms over her chest. "Look, I don't need your pity. I have friends. Many friends. I think Corey is the one who's lonely. He misses his dad, and this is his attempt to—to—" She exhaled sharply. "Frankly, I don't know what he's trying to do."

"Divorced?"

"What?"

"Are you divorced?" Of course he already knew the answer. He'd learned quite a lot about Alana from Hannah. But he wanted to loosen her up, get her to talk to him.

She hugged herself tighter. "Yes."

"For very long?"

Her chin went up. "Long enough."

"I'm not trying to pry. Just trying to understand where Corey's coming from."

Her gaze narrowed. "Why?"

"What do you mean, why?"

"Why would you care?" She held his gaze. "You're a grown man with a life of your own. Are you planning on playing ball with him after school? Or teaching him how to skateboard or do other things friends do together?"

Sean made a face. What the hell was she getting at?

"Look," she said, her expression softening, "Corey has already had enough disappointment in his life. If he is looking for a father figure, he doesn't need to have a part-time playmate that's going to disappoint him again."

"Ah, so you have me all figured out."

She sighed. "You're young, I have to assume single, and good-looking. I'm sure you have a busy enough social schedule that you don't need a little boy anxiously waiting for your phone calls."

He straightened. So she thought he was good-looking. That was a start. "How do you know I'm not divorced myself, and that I'm not a single father raising my son?"

She reared her head back. "Are you?"

"Well, no."

She rolled her eyes.

"I'm just saying you shouldn't be so judgmental."

"That's not it at all. I wouldn't blame you for wanting to go bar hopping at night, or…" She waved a frustrated hand. "Or whatever it is that young single people do."

Sean studied her face. "How old are you?"

She shrank back. "Why?"

"Because you're acting like you're over the hill."

"How I'm acting is like a responsible adult. The way a parent is supposed to behave."

"Not that. I admire the fact you're concerned about Corey. But what's all this stuff about 'whatever it is that young single people do?'"

"I didn't sound that condescending."

"Wanna bet?"

"Sorry," she murmured, her gaze straying toward the stage. "I think they're bidding on the last item."

"Good. I could do with less noise."

She looked at him again, her eyes wary. "I'd better go find Corey."

"He's with Hannah. He's fine."

Annoyance flickered in her face. "I'll be the judge as to whether my son is fine or not."

"Right. You're the judge of a lot of things."

"Look, I said I was sorry for *generalizing*. Take it or leave it."

Sean smiled, liking her no-nonsense attitude. She was right. He'd done his share of bar-hopping since living in Seattle, and he'd met several young ladies who'd interested him enough that he'd taken them out a few times. But they all seemed to be part of the café latte crowd, more interested in partying and orchestrating their lives around their careers.

He was more the strong black coffee type. At twenty-nine, he figured he ought to start seriously thinking about settling down. No question he wanted a family. He loved kids.

Alana didn't seem to be the type of woman he usually met. She had a great career, but her son was obviously her priority. Well balanced. He liked that.

"It was really nice meeting you, Sean." She started to offer her hand, but hesitated. "Truly. And I appreciate your patience with Corey."

"No problem."

"Okay." She ran her palms down the front of her skirt. "I'd better go round him up. It's past his bedtime."

"Sure."

"Okay then." She gave him a small smile and turned to go.

"Alana?"

She stopped and looked at him.

"Sunday night a good night for you?"

"Excuse me?"

"For our date."

Her lips parted in surprise. Nice lips. The lower one full, the upper one bow-shaped. "I thought we settled that."

"We did." He shrugged and tried to hold back a smile. "I thought you didn't want to disappoint Corey."

"THIS IS RIDICULOUS." Alana pushed a hand through her hair, her fingers snagging on a nasty tangle. No wonder. She'd fidgeted with it unmercifully for the past half hour while she'd chatted over coffee with Hannah. Her friend had dropped by early that morning to make sure Alana was not angry about the fact that the two day care partners had helped Corey arrange to have Sean take his mom out. "Why should I go on a date with a man my son coerced into asking me out?"

Hannah pursed her lips, thinking for a moment. "He didn't actually ask you out. He bought you."

"Oh, yeah. That makes it better."

Hannah grinned. "Don't you think he's hot?"

Alana let her head fall to the table and pressed her forehead against the cool oak. Why was she even having this conversation?

"Tell me the truth."

"What?"

"Don't you think he's a hottie?"

"He has some nice qualities."

Hannah laughed as she drained the rest of her coffee into the sink and then rinsed out her mug. "Honey, you can be as stubborn as you want, but I saw the way you sized him up last night."

"I didn't size him up." Alana glared at her friend. "I was concerned about who my son was hanging out with."

"Right."

"Just put that in the dishwasher." She rubbed her tired eyes. "I think there's room."

Hannah got rid of the mug, then went to take Alana's, but she shook her head. She needed much more caffeine. Mega amounts of the stuff. She'd barely slept last night, and she had a collie with a limp to examine at noon and Mildred Golden's schizophrenic Chihuahua right after.

"Look, go out with him tomorrow night…have a good time." Hannah returned to her seat opposite

Alana, and patted her hand. "I promise it's not a crime."

"You don't understand. I have Corey to worry about."

"I understand more than you think."

Alana noted the flicker of sadness in the other woman's blue eyes and decided it was time to lighten things up. She knew Hannah hadn't had an easy time of it. Nine years ago she'd given up her baby in the belief he'd be better off in a two-parent family.

But after all these years they'd been reunited, and now Hannah had her son, Adam, and Adam's father, Jack. One big happy family. Even better, Hannah was pregnant again.

Alana leaned back and folded her arms across her chest. "If Sean is such a hot ticket, why didn't you ever date him?"

"Aren't you forgetting about one small detail, like my husband?"

"Sean's been around awhile. I'm talking about before Jack."

Hannah made a wry face. "Because I was just as uptight about taking the risk as you are."

"For goodness' sakes, I haven't been divorced that long. What do you expect?"

"It's been well over a year since the legal part…longer since the emotional separation. And how many dates have you had?"

Alana shifted uncomfortably. There was more to it than the divorce. If Brad had decided his career precluded a family, or that he just wasn't ready to settle down, maybe it would have been different. She wouldn't feel so beaten and fragile. But he'd found *her* lacking. He'd sought fulfillment in another woman's bed.

"I really don't want to talk about this anymore." She got up to get more coffee, in need of escape more than caffeine. "Tell me about the auction. Did you raise as much money as you'd hoped?"

Hannah's eyes lit up—Alana's love life, or lack thereof, obviously forgotten. "We kicked butt, as my son would say. Everyone was so generous with their bids, it was unbelievable."

"That's terrific." Of course Alana was happy for their success, but she had an ulterior motive. Forrester Square Day Care provided wonderful child care and a stimulating learning environment for Corey while she worked. "I take it you have enough to pay off the debt?"

"Alexandra is still crunching numbers and making sure all the auction expenses are covered, but it looks really good." She glanced at her watch. "In fact, I've got to run. The advertising for the auction was totally coordinated by Debbie North. She's a reporter for the *Seattle Post-Intelligencer.* You know her, right?"

"Alexandra has spoken of her, that's all." Alana left it at that. From what she knew, the reporter had befriended the three partners around the time Katherine's father, Louis Kinard, had gotten out of prison.

He'd been charged with embezzling from the company he owned with Hannah's father, Kenneth Richards, and Alexandra's father, Jonathan Webber. The charge had also included the sale of their company's sensitive computer software—programs designed for military use—on the black market. The scandal had rocked Seattle at the time. Like other reporters, Debbie North had been eager to get the scoop. Alana didn't blame the woman for being ambitious, but she hoped Hannah and Alexandra weren't overly trusting.

"Anyway, I didn't mean to stay so long. Alexandra and I are going over to Debbie's apartment to take her some flowers and wine as a thank-you." Hannah hesitated at the back door. "Go out with Sean tomorrow night. The worst that can happen is that you'll have a miserable time and you won't see him again."

Alana sighed. "Right."

Hannah grinned. "But I promise, you two will have a fabulous time. Monday morning I want all the details."

Slumping in her chair, Alana watched her leave. Hannah meant well, of course, but she didn't understand. No one truly did, and Alana certainly didn't expect anyone to comprehend the betrayal she'd felt after Brad left.

A date.

That's what tomorrow night would be. No getting around it. Jeez. Even when she'd been single, she hadn't liked to date much. Now she was thirty-two, the idea was even less appealing.

Darn it. She ought to call and tell Sean to forget it. Corey would get over any fleeting disappointment. She could even fib and tell him she had to postpone the date because one of the animals she boarded was ill.

The thought of lying to her son caused her chest to tighten. She pushed out of her chair to get one last cup of coffee before going back to the clinic and waiting for her next appointment.

The phone rang.

Maybe it was Sean. He could have had second thoughts.

She hurried to answer it, pausing when she reached for the receiver to check the caller ID. It was Brad. Phoning from Sheila's. The worm.

Alana took a deep calming breath before picking up. "Hello." She sounded annoyed. She hadn't meant to.

"Hey, baby, what's going on?"

"Don't call me baby." *Save it for Sheila.* She held her tongue, though there were a dozen things she wanted to say. "I left a message on your answering machine earlier in the week."

"I know. That's why I'm calling."

"Silly me. I thought maybe you wanted to talk to your son." She bit her lower lip, briefly closing her eyes at the childish sarcasm.

"Feel better?" he asked in a cocky tone that took the sting out of her self-reproach.

Alana took a big gulp of pride. "I apologize. I'd called because I want to arrange for a weekend so you can come see Corey."

"You mean I have to drive all the way over there?"

She shook her head but kept her cool. "He misses you, Brad. He wants to see you."

"Look, honey, you're the one who moved away.

Why should I be inconvenienced? Why can't you bring him here?''

"You're off on weekends. I have clinic hours on Saturday.''

"So, it won't kill you to close shop for one day.''

It took every ounce of willpower not to remind him that if he were dependable with the child support checks, she wouldn't have to work six days a week. And then Corey popped his head in the back door and maternal desperation promptly replaced any animosity toward Brad.

She winked at her son and in a much friendlier voice said, "Okay, tell me when and I'll arrange to take the weekend off.''

Brad hesitated. "I'm going to have to get back to you on that.''

She struggled to keep her tone light. "When?''

"I don't know. Next week.''

Damn him. It would be another month before he called. "Monday?''

"Look, I gotta go. Sheila's waiting.''

"Of course.'' She smiled at Corey. "I'll talk to you later.'' Brad had hung up before she finished talking, but she kept up the pretense for Corey's benefit.

She replaced the receiver, her smile intact. "How about some lunch?''

"Who was that?'' he asked with a mischievous gleam in his eyes that gave her hope he didn't suspect the caller had been his father.

"What did I tell you about being nosy, young man? Now, how about a tuna sandwich?''

His grin widened. "That was Sean, huh?"

Relieved, she gave in to the little fib. "Yes."

"Cool beans. What time is he picking you up?"

Darn it. Corey looked so pleased. How could she weasel out now? She forced a smile. "Tomorrow. At six."

CHAPTER FOUR

"WHAT IN THE WORLD—?" Debbie North stepped back to let Alexandra and Hannah into her apartment, taking the enormous bunch of fresh cut flowers Hannah handed her. "What are these for?"

Alexandra passed her the bottle of Clos Des Jacobins 1998 and shut the door behind them. "They're for you."

"Why?" Debbie sniffed a red carnation.

"Because you're a wonder." Alexandra reached into the pink tote bag she carried and brought out the crystal vase Hannah had picked up on her way home from Alana's house. "If you point me in the direction of the kitchen, I'll get some water, then clip the ends of the stems. That way they'll last longer."

Debbie looked helplessly at Hannah as Alexandra set off without directions. "What's going on?"

"Last night. The auction. The fair." Hannah couldn't stop smiling. "To say it was a success would be an understatement. It was awesome."

Debbie chuckled. "I take it you made a few bucks."

Hannah nodded. "Thanks to you."

"I didn't do a thing."

"You did all the advertising and coordinating of items—and on very short notice."

"Big deal." Frowning, she studied the label on the wine. "Very nice. But way too extravagant. I hope you made a hell of a lot of money. I'm sorry I couldn't be there."

Hannah gave her a teasing smile. She liked Debbie, even knowing she'd obviously befriended Hannah and Alexandra and Katherine in order to get the inside scoop on Louis Kinard's release from prison. Hannah didn't begrudge the reporter trying to do her job, and over time, their friendship had evolved.

"Alexandra did the final paperwork this afternoon. We have enough to pay off the loan."

"Oh, my God, that's terrific." Debbie gave her a one-armed hug, still juggling the wine and flowers. "Now you can get those greedy bastards off your back."

"Hey, Katherine borrowed the money for the day care from Jordan. When he died, his heirs had every right to call in the loan." Hannah didn't like the way the Edwards heirs had gone about their demands, but she'd accepted it. Just as Katherine and Alexandra had done.

Debbie sniffed. "As if they need the dough."

"It doesn't matter now." Hannah grinned. "We're off the hook. Largely thanks to you."

Alexandra reappeared. "I'm going to need these," she said as she grabbed the bouquet out of Debbie's hand. "I'll bring the flowers into the living room when I'm done arranging them. Go sit."

Debbie and Hannah both laughed. "I guess I don't

need to tell you where the scissors are,'' Debbie called out.

"Nope.''

"You know Alexandra,'' Hannah said. "Determined and resourceful.''

"One of the many things I like about her.'' Debbie set down the wine on a console table next to an interesting piece of mauve pottery with etchings of coyotes. "Come on in to the living room. Let Alexandra think we've been obedient.''

Hannah followed her into a small but attractive room decorated in a southwestern theme. The walls were cream, the sofa and rugs a mix of mauve and pale turquoise. Lots of pottery was scattered around. Not the ordinary variety that you'd pick up in a furniture store or gallery, but unusual pieces that Debbie might have found during her travels.

"This is terrific. I love the way you've decorated.'' Hannah stopped at an end table to study what appeared to be a religious relic, a misshapen cross of sorts. "Did you collect all of these things yourself?''

"Some of them I found when I was down in New Mexico and Arizona looking for a job after college. But the more unique pottery I inherited from my grandmother.'' She picked up a hand woven throw off the sofa and gave it a fond look. "She made this.''

"It's beautiful.'' Hannah scanned the room, which was perfectly decorated and free of clutter, unlike the attached dining room. It had been turned into an office, and papers and news clippings were strewn across the table.

Debbie half sighed, half laughed. "It's a mess, but if you move a single sheet of paper, my entire filing system goes kaput."

"I know all about that," Hannah said absently, her thoughts going back to the religious artifacts on the table. "You know, my mom has always had a fondness for southwestern decor, and that's how she had her vacation home in the San Juan Islands decorated. But she's getting rid of a lot of her stuff. If you're interested, I can see what's left from the garage sale she had."

Debbie's eyebrows rose. "Somehow I can't see your mother interested in anything southwestern."

"Yeah, I know. It doesn't seem like her usual style." Hannah tried not to get defensive. Olivia Richards was a well-known interior designer with a high-end clientele and a streak of snobbery she did little to conceal. Sometimes even Hannah didn't understand her. "But she does have some interesting pieces, even a few religious icons like you have over there on the table."

"Really? I'd love to have a look."

"There's some African masks, too, but they wouldn't go well in here. But the other stuff, like the oversize wooden rosary beads or the crystal cross might be—"

"A crystal cross?"

Hannah nodded, sensing Debbie's excitement.

"What does it look like?"

"A cross."

Debbie didn't laugh. "How big?"

"I don't know." Hannah shrugged. "Maybe about so," she said, parting her hands approximately ten inches. "But I can't remember for sure."

Debbie hurried toward the dining room table and searched through a stack of newspaper clippings. Her movements were brisk, almost frantic, and made Hannah uneasy.

"Look at this," Debbie said, handing her a newspaper article. Protected by a plastic sleeve, the paper was yellowing. "Is this the cross?"

Hannah squinted at the fuzzy picture. "I can't tell for sure but I don't think so." Her gaze went to the caption. This was the cross stolen from Our Lady of Mercy the same night as the house fire that had killed both of Alexandra's parents.

Hannah shivered. That was the thing about Debbie. She was obsessed with Louis Kinard's arrest, which had happened around the same time as the fire. Jonathan Webber had been Louis's partner, along with Hannah's own father. Although Louis had spent twenty years in prison, he had never admitted any guilt, and even after such a long time, Louis's release the previous fall had caused a media frenzy. Details of the case and the fire were still being rehashed.

Hannah quickly handed the clipping back to Debbie. Alexandra was suffering nightmares about that night, and Hannah didn't want to upset her. "I doubt it's the same cross. In fact, I'm sure it can't be. After all, what would my mother be doing with it?"

A faraway look came into Debbie's eyes, and Hannah thought she heard her murmur, "Good question."

"WOW, MOM, YOU LOOK PHAT." Corey circled her, his eyes wide and shining. "Really awesome."

Good thing Alana was familiar with the hip term *phat,* or she'd have likely crumpled into a heap. Corey had heard the latest word for "cool" a few months ago, and even if it wasn't the most current slang, her son tried to worm it into as many sentences as he could.

"I'm not dressed any differently," she told him. "Sean and I are only going to dinner."

"And a movie, too. Right?"

"Maybe."

His expression fell. "I thought that was part of the date."

She cringed at the word. All day she'd told herself it was just dinner with a friend. Well, Corey's friend. "We probably will go to a movie."

His triumphant grin made her want to ground him for a week. "Hannah says I can even spend the night with her and Jack and Adam."

Alana let out a shaky laugh. "I guarantee you I won't be out that late."

"But just in case."

She shuddered. Being single again really stunk. The digital alarm clock beside her bed flipped to five-fifty. Hannah was supposed to have picked Corey up five minutes ago. Maybe something had come up. Maybe she wouldn't be able to watch Corey, and Alana would have to cancel with Sean. Her mood lifted.

The doorbell rang and the butterflies in her stomach started to jitterbug.

"I'll get it." Corey ran ahead of her.

"You know you're not supposed to answer the door without me," she called out as she took one last look in the mirror in case it was Sean.

The reflex irritated her. It was only dinner. Not a date.

She started to pull away from her reflection but noticed a few strands of hair were out of place. She tucked them back into the French braid and gave herself a disgusted look.

"Mom!" Corey's voice rose with excitement. "It's Sean."

Her stomach fluttered again, and she reminded herself this wasn't a date. She walked out of the bedroom and down the short hall, then paused before stepping into the living room. As soon as she saw him their eyes met, and he did a slow perusal of her all the way down to her toes. Nothing insolent or obnoxious, and when their eyes met again, the appreciative gleam she found in his warmed her ego.

Good to his word, he'd dressed casually in jeans and a light blue long-sleeved western shirt. Surprising herself, she took an equally long look at him, her gaze lingering on the two sharp creases up the front legs of his jeans. Had he actually ironed them?

This time when she met his amused eyes, her cheeks heated up. Should she explain that she was only looking at the creases in his jeans? Oh, brother, the evening was not off to a good start.

"Hi," she said simply, glancing at her son. She was

doing this for him. If she just kept that in mind, she'd be okay.

"Hi yourself. You look really nice."

She shrugged a shoulder. "My usual dress."

"Yeah, but she's got stuff around her eyes." Corey squinted at her. "It looks good, Mom."

No wonder some animals ate their young. "Obviously Hannah isn't here yet," she said quickly. "So I can't leave. If you want to cancel, I perfectly—"

"Relax." He smiled. "I'm early. Not very considerate of me, and I do apologize. I misjudged the traffic."

"You wanna see my train collection?" Corey asked, redeeming himself and motioning Sean to follow him. "My grandpa gives me a new one every Christmas."

"Sure." Sean winked at Alana, then strode after Corey. Unabashedly she used the opportunity to check out his butt. Damn fine by any standard.

"Hey."

She spun toward Hannah's voice. Her friend stood at the still-open door, a knowing smile tugging at her lips.

"Sorry, I'm late. I had some errands to run and it took longer than I expected."

Alana waved a hand for her to come in. "No problem. In fact, if tonight isn't good, I'm sure Sean will understand."

"Nice try. I'm fine." She looked tired, a little edgy. "Where is the little rascal?"

"Seriously, Hannah, maybe we should make it another night."

"Why?" She sounded impatient, not at all like herself. "Is Sean here?"

"In Corey's room, looking at his train collection."

"I saw a Corvette in the drive. Sean normally drives a pickup. Probably trying to impress you."

"A Corvette definitely wouldn't impress me."

Hannah gave her a weary smile. "Sorry if I sounded snappish. Debbie North is still—" She shrugged. "We stayed too long at her place yesterday and it put me behind schedule the entire weekend."

Alana didn't comment on how preoccupied Hannah seemed. She only smiled. "We shouldn't be late."

"I told Corey he could stay the night."

"We're just having dinner."

Reaching over, Hannah squeezed her hand. "Give him a chance. He's really a great guy."

Sheesh. Why the heck was everyone suddenly worried about her love life? "I made some brownies. Let me go get them while you call Corey."

"Just what my thighs need. But I won't turn them down. Alana?" Hannah stopped at the beginning of the hall. "You look great."

If Alana's cheeks got any more heated tonight, she'd end up with permanent sunburn. She opened her mouth to protest that she often wore long skirts, that she hadn't done anything special for tonight. But that was a lie, and Hannah would call her on it. So Alana just shut up.

"ARE YOU SURE THIS restaurant is okay with you?" Sean asked once they were seated with menus in front of them.

"Of course." She'd thought it sounded good when he suggested the popular steakhouse. "I've heard lots of good comments about it."

"Okay." He sounded skeptical.

She figured she knew why. "I'm a veterinarian, not a vegetarian."

His grin was wide and immediate. "I know, but you could have been a vegetarian."

"Yes, but then I would have suggested another kind of restaurant."

"Point taken." Looking pleased, he transferred his attention to the menu. "I'm starved. I want everything."

She smiled and watched him study the list of appetizers, his absorption and slight changes of expression fascinating. When the waiter arrived to take their drink orders, she was ridiculously pleased that he asked for iced tea, remarking that he had to go to work tomorrow.

That small detail had never stopped Brad. If any of his friends called him to go have a beer, he'd be halfway out the door before he hung up, no matter what time of day it was.

"Want to share the artichoke and spinach dip?" he asked, still seriously studying the list. "And maybe the potato skins?"

"Both?"

He glanced up from the menu, his hazel eyes looking almost brown in the dim lighting. "Why not?"

She laughed. "You are hungry. Unless you're only having appetizers."

"Yeah, right." He went back to the menu. "That twenty-ounce porterhouse has my name on it."

"No way."

The look of sheer surprise on his face was her answer. "I'm a growing boy."

Well, he was sure right about that. Technically, he was a man, but Alana knew better. Guys didn't grow up until their midthirties, if then. If Brad hadn't been example enough, her father had done his share of moronic things well into his late fifties.

She'd been too young to understand at the time, but as a mother herself, she now recognized the childish stunts he'd pulled that had her mom sending him to spend the night on the couch on a semiregular basis.

"What about you?" he asked, snapping her out of her musings. "What looks good?"

She stared at the menu. "I'll share the dip and potato skins with you."

"I meant for your entrée."

"So did I."

Disappointment flickered in his face and he set the menu aside. "I didn't figure you for one of those women who only pick at two olives and say they're full."

"Really?" She smiled sweetly. Might as well nip this whole let's get to know each other thing in the bud. "In your vast knowledge of my personal life, what did you figure out about me?"

He didn't bat an eye at her sarcasm. "Well, let's see...I know you're a good mom because Corey obviously adores you and would move heaven and earth for you if he could." A slow smile lifted his lips. "I also know you're not too permissive, because he was so worried about you nabbing him at the auction, he about dislocated his neck looking over his shoulder."

She sighed. "But it didn't stop him, did it?"

"Is this really so bad?"

She met his eyes, startled by the way he'd lowered his voice.

"Being here, having dinner with me. Is it that bad?"

"Of course not." She removed the utensils from atop her napkin and spread the soft white cloth across her lap, keeping her gaze lowered.

"Look, I know divorce sucks. I've never been married, but if you're committed in a relationship with someone, to me, it's the same thing."

"No, it's not." She hadn't meant to say that. She didn't even want to have this conversation with him. Rarely did she discuss the divorce or her personal life. And when she did, it was with someone with whom she felt close and safe.

"Why not?"

She toyed with the hem of her napkin, stalling, hoping he'd change the subject.

"Seriously, I'd like to hear why you think a personal commitment to someone you love is different from marriage.''

"If there was no difference, why would the institution of marriage have evolved at all?"

He shrugged. "There are a lot of legal reasons, laws that preclude single people from enjoying the same benefits as married couples. The feelings between two people shouldn't be any different. And if the relationship disintegrates, it hurts like hell whether you're married or not."

Alana didn't miss the pain that flashed in his eyes. He'd been through his own personal hell. As curious as she was, she wouldn't ask. None of her business. And she was none of his.

"So," she said matter-of-factly, "you don't believe in marriage."

"Wrong."

Confused, she frowned. "But you just said that the vows are for legal reasons only."

"No, what I explained was why the institution evolved."

She thought about it for a moment. "Okay, but—"

The waiter arrived with their drinks and to take their food orders. Sean ordered like a pregnant women eating for triplets. Alana opted for soup and salad.

As soon as the waiter left, Sean grunted. "This is a steakhouse and you order lettuce and soup."

She fixed him with the kind of stare that sent Corey scurrying for shelter. "Did I tell you what to order?"

Sean laughed. "Touché."

A smile tugged at her lips and she shrugged. "I'm

a grazer. I like to eat a little of this and a little of that so I basically eat all day long rather than three meals.''

''See, there you go. I know something else about you now.''

Laughing softly, she shook her head. ''No kidding. I just spelled it out for you.''

''Not about your eating habits. I'm talking about how you stand up for your opinion and don't just sit there and look pretty.''

The admiration in his eyes both pleased and unnerved her. He did possess an awful lot of insight, especially for someone his age. More than insight, he seemed to really contemplate life.

She frowned at the sudden thought that she didn't actually know how old he was. Around thirty, she'd guess, but he'd worked outdoors a lot, and the crinkly lines at the corner of his eyes gave him a weathered look, so it was hard to tell.

''What are you thinking?'' Over the rim of his glass, he studied her with intense interest. Even while he took a sip of his ice tea, he held her gaze.

She blinked. ''Nothing in particular,'' she murmured, feeling her cheeks heat up.

One side of his mouth lifted.

Alana rested her forearms on the table and leaned forward. ''Okay, I have a question for you.''

''Shoot.''

''When should a committed monogamous relationship advance to marriage?''

''When both partners are sure the other will make a good parent.''

More than a little surprised, she sank back in her chair. "I'm not sure I follow. Are you saying the first part is a test of some sort?"

His forehead creased and he seemed to give the thought serious consideration. "Not really. The first part is about getting to know one another, deciding that you're willing to promise your exclusivity." He paused, his face thoughtful. "But raising kids is a serious responsibility. If you want them, and you suddenly realize this other person wouldn't make a good mother or father, then…" He shrugged. "Marriage isn't an option."

Alana didn't know what to think. "You would drop someone, a woman you cared about, because you didn't see her as a good mother."

"Probably sounds callous, but, yeah I'd have to part company with her."

"Well, that's certainly honest."

He gave her a wry smile. "But dirty."

"No, not really." She admired the fact that he wanted to be a responsible parent, but… "Heck, I don't know what to think."

"Yeah." He rolled his shoulders, and for the first time, seemed a little uncomfortable. "Life's decisions can get complicated. I wonder where the appetizers are."

Glad he seemed ready to change the subject, she took a cold sip of ice tea. She'd have to be crazy to get into any kind of deep conversation with him. This was just for one night. She'd gone out with him as she'd promised.

But darn it. She was really starting to like him.

CHAPTER FIVE

"WHEN ARE YOU GOING OUT with him again?" Corey balanced two filled water dishes on a tray for the black Lab and cocker spaniel that were staying in the kennel for the night.

Alana put away the rabies vaccine she'd just received and locked the cabinet. "How many times are you going to ask me that question?"

He stopped when water started to slosh from the bowls and looked at her. "But you didn't answer me."

"Honey, I told you what a nice dinner we had."

"But you didn't even go to a movie or nothing."

"Anything. A movie or anything." She sighed and lifted one of the bowls off the tray and set it in front of the black Lab. "We both had to get up early and go to work this morning."

"So that means you still have to go to a movie another night, right?"

"Corey, why are you so anxious to get rid of me?"

His eyes widened in horror. "I don't wanna get rid of you, Mommy. I just want you to be happy."

Alana dropped to his level, balancing herself with one knee on the floor. She took the tray with the other bowl from him, set it aside, then hugged him to her. "I am happy. I love being here with you."

"But not happy like you were before."

She swallowed. It had been a lot easier being happy before she'd found out Brad was sleeping with Sheila. "That's not true. I'm busier now because my practice here is so new and I don't have time to do more fun things. But that will change. I know. Let's go to the zoo next Sunday."

He shrugged his narrow shoulders.

"Hey." She pulled away from him and forced up his chin. "You love the zoo."

He only shrugged again, his eyes downcast.

"Heck, I'm crazy about the zoo. I wish someone would take me."

The voice came from behind, startling her, and she almost landed on her fanny.

Corey's eyes lit up as he looked over her head. "Sean."

"Hey, you, what's going on?" He came to stand beside Alana and stuck out his hand. "Want a lift?"

She thought about declining but figured it would only make matters worse. She gave him her hand and he hauled her to her feet. When he didn't seem anxious to let go, she pulled away and muttered, "Thanks."

"No problem, Doc." He turned to Corey. "I didn't see you at the center today."

"You were there?"

"I had to finish tearing down the stage from Friday night."

"I could have helped you." Corey grinned. "I'm pretty strong."

Furrowing his brow, Sean squeezed Corey's bicep.

"Yeah, you're pretty strong, all right. You must be working out."

"Huh?" Corey giggled and wriggled out of Sean's flexing grip.

"You know, pumping iron."

"Oh, yeah." Corey nodded solemnly, and Sean laughed.

Alana shook her head, trying not to smile. "Okay, sport, how about you finish your chores while you gab."

Corey rolled his eyes at Sean, but went to fill another set of bowls with kibble.

"What can I do for you?" she asked, and Sean's eyes sparked with amusement.

"Nothing. I was in the neighborhood and saw the clinic light on, so I stopped by."

"You don't live around here."

"About five miles. The grocery store I shop at is around the corner." He frowned suddenly. "Why are you looking at me like that?"

She moved to the sink and vigorously began washing her hands. "I didn't expect you to live in such a suburban neighborhood."

That startled a laugh out of him. "Why not?"

She shrugged. "I figured you'd live in an apartment in the city. You know, closer to the action." She turned to grab the towel but he beat her to it.

He handed her the white towel. "What kind of action?"

She focused on drying every inch of skin from her forearms to the tips of her fingers. When she finally looked up, Corey stared at the two of them with far too much interest. "You need to go wash up for dinner."

"But—"

"Now, Corey."

He took a step back toward the clinic door. "Can Sean stay for dinner?"

Alana's head began to throb. "I'm sure he already has plans."

"Nope, he sure doesn't." Sean smiled. "But if I'm intruding—"

"Mom doesn't care. She says my friends are always welcome to eat with me. Huh, Mom?"

"Of course." Great, now she'd be the bad guy. She gave Sean a pathetically pleading look. "But the thing is, I don't have anything planned. Not a traditional dinner, anyway."

"No problem."

She gave him a grateful smile for realizing tonight wouldn't be a good time.

"I have some groceries in the car," he said, digging keys out of his jeans' pocket. "I'll whip up something for all of us."

"Oh, no, that isn't necessary."

"Cool." Corey's grin stretched from ear to ear. "I'll help."

SEAN WASN'T THE LEAST surprised that she had chicken nearly thawed in the refrigerator, or that a box of instant mashed potatoes was sitting on the counter near the stove. He knew she'd been trying to get rid of him.

Tough. He didn't scare that easily.

He found some milk and butter in the refrigerator and brought in a bag of potatoes from his car, along with fresh spinach and a few other goodies.

It wasn't like he was trying to jump her bones. Not yet, anyway. He just wanted to get to know her. If she'd relax for two minutes, she might enjoy getting to know him, too.

He knew she didn't dislike him. If he had the slightest doubt, he'd back off. The divorce had obviously done a number on her, but she was too young and smart and pretty to shut herself off.

"What do you want me to do?" Corey asked, eyeing the spinach with suspicion.

"How about you scrub the potato skins?"

"With what?"

"Here." Sean got out a vegetable scrubber he'd found in the utility drawer. "Like this, but we'll have to get you a stool to stand on so you can do it in the sink."

"What's that for?" Corey indicated the spinach with a tilt of his head.

"We're planting it." He'd almost said "smoking it," but remembered who his audience was just in time.

"Really?"

Sean chuckled. "We're going to eat it."

Corey wrinkled his nose. "But it's green."

"Very good." On the floor in front of the sink, he

put the low kitchen stool he'd found in the pantry. "Here you go. I'm going to need those potatoes pretty quick."

"Mom won't make me eat it," he muttered as he stepped up and wrestled with his first potato.

"She won't have to. It'll be so delicious, you'll want to eat it." Sean hid a smile at Corey's comical look of disbelief. "In fact, you'll want seconds, but there probably won't be any left because everyone loves my spinach salad."

Corey didn't say another word. But the skeptical look didn't leave his face as he continued attacking the potatoes. Sean put some water on to boil and then got out a frying pan and some bacon.

By the time Alana walked in, he'd already fried the bacon crisp and had the potatoes boiling. She took a look at the crowded counters and gasped.

"Are you finished in the clinic?"

She nodded, her attention still glued to the stove. "You're making mashed potatoes from scratch?"

"Yep."

"Why didn't you use instant?"

"I wanted to impress you with my culinary skills."

Their eyes met, and when she saw that he was teasing, she smiled. "Hate to tell you, but Betty Crocker impresses me."

"I helped." Corey moved his stool closer to the stove. "Want me to stir anything?"

"No, thanks," Sean said quickly, and scooped up the stool before Corey could get near the heat. "How about some lemonade?"

"With sugar?"

Sean glanced at Alana and she gave him a slight nod.

"Yep, with sugar."

"I'll get us each a glass," Alana said. "I wouldn't want to impede your progress."

"Hungry, huh?"

"I am now. What's that in the oven I smell?"

"Chicken."

She blushed and turned to get three glasses out of the cupboard. "Did I have some thawed out? I couldn't remember."

He got the pitcher of lemonade out of the refrigerator and took it to her.

She tensed and moved back a little. "Would you rather have a beer?"

"If you have one, that would be great."

"But tomorrow's a work day," she reminded him.

He shrugged. "It's still early. One won't hurt me."

"Right." Something odd sparked in her eyes, something like disappointment or annoyance, which didn't make sense, because her lips twitched in a brief smile. "What can I do?"

"Set the table."

"I can do that." She handed Corey his lemonade and left the other two glasses on the counter.

"Hey, Mom, now you get to set three places again."

Alana gave him a sharp look.

Corey either didn't notice or ignored it. "You know, without getting all mad at yourself."

She slid Sean a wary glance. "Go wash up, Corey."

"I did that already." He turned to Sean with a sad expression. "Sometimes she forgets and sets a place at the table for Daddy, and then she gets really—"

"Darn it." Sean snapped his fingers, effectively cutting the boy off. "I forgot to bring in the rolls from my car." He dug out his keys. "Think you can get them for me?"

Corey looked at his mother for permission.

"The car is in the driveway, close to the house." He waited for her to nod and then handed Corey the keys. "You just have to push this button on the remote to open the door."

Corey nodded, appearing eager to run the errand.

"You understand?" Sean asked, crouching in front of the little boy so that he had his full attention. "Tell me what you're going to do."

"I'm gonna go get the rolls," Corey said, frowning.

A sudden thought occurred to Sean. "What kind of rolls?"

The boy glanced at his mother and shrugged.

Alana and Sean both laughed, but quickly sobered when embarrassment clouded Corey's face.

"Do you know what a roll is?" Sean asked gently.

Corey stared back without a word.

"Honey, a roll is the kind of bread we eat with dinner," Alana explained.

"No, we don't. We only eat bread when we're having a sandwich at lunch."

She sighed. "We eat rolls on holidays. Now, hurry before the rest of dinner is ready."

He scampered off, and Sean started to rise, but a cramp in his left thigh stopped him. He massaged the knot of tension for a few seconds, then looked up at Alana. "How about returning the favor?"

"Pardon?"

He stretched out his hand. "Give me a lift."

She looked as if he'd asked her to grab a bunch of poison ivy. Tentatively she grasped his hand, first using one hand and then two to pull him to his feet.

Her skin was incredibly soft, especially since, as a vet, she had to be constantly washing her hands. The aroma of her shampoo drifted up to him, filling his nostrils with the flowery scent and a surprise longing in his heart.

"I'd better set the table," she murmured, moving back until the counter blocked her way. "Thanks for not embarrassing Corey."

Her remark caught him off guard. "Heck, why would I do that?"

"You didn't tease him. Some men find nothing wrong with that. They think it builds character or some such foolishness." She turned, giving him her back, and opened the cupboard.

Automatically he reached around her to help bring down plates. Her hair smelled damn good. *She* smelled good. "Kids nowadays have enough peer pressure and harassment."

"You don't think teasing and goading are part of male childhood development."

"Hell, no. All that will do is give us a generation of bullies."

She grinned. Sincere, uninhibited, her smile lit up the room. "You're wasting your talent wielding a hammer. You should have a big office with a couch where clients lie down for two hundred bucks an hour."

Like he hadn't heard that before. Sean took the plates to the table and went to check on the potatoes. "Nothing wrong with making one's living with a hammer."

"Of course not. I didn't mean that."

"No problem."

"Sean."

He pierced a piece of potato with a fork. It was ready, so he drained the water from the pot.

"Sean, please."

"Honest." He laughed. "No problem. It's forgotten already." He knew she'd meant nothing. In a way, she'd been complimenting him. He was just touchy.

"Would you at least look at me?"

He turned toward her with a grin. "Glad to."

Not even a hint of a smile at the corners of her mouth. "I've said something thoughtless and hurt your feelings. So, yes, there is a problem. But I'm very sorry."

Her troubled eyes tugged at him. She wasn't classically pretty but she had the best lips and a sexy way of pursing them when she was anxious or upset.

"Alana." He touched the tip of her chin. "It's okay. If I reacted, it had nothing to do with you. Old baggage, that's all."

She stared back, a little fear, a little excitement in

her eyes. "I, uh—" She softly cleared her throat and then moistened her lips. "Thank you."

He had no idea what she was thanking him for, but when he tilted his head toward hers, she moved a fraction closer.

"Hey, Sean, I've got the rolls." Corey's voice came like a blast of cold water and they jumped apart.

ALANA HAD INSISTED ON cleanup duty since the guys cooked. Sean had started to argue and then realized the Seattle Mariners' game had started. So he and Corey planted themselves in front of the television while she loaded the dishwasher and wiped down the counters and stove.

How she'd managed to eat two helpings, she had no idea. No, that wasn't true. She knew it was because Sean was such a darn good cook. No broiled, dried out chicken breasts tonight. He'd assured her the sauce was low fat, as hard as it was to believe. Apparently his sister had given him the recipe when he'd gone to visit her and her family last year.

While she dried the frying pan, Alana peeked into the family room. Corey and Sean sat side by side on the couch, their attention glued to the TV.

"All right!"

Sean's sudden yell startled her. Corey's whoop echoed him and they turned to each other and high-fived.

Her heart fluttered.

It should have been Brad sitting there with his son. But Brad had always been too busy watching the game in bars with his friends.

She forced her thoughts away from anything depressing and focused on her son. He'd been so happy all evening. Even his appetite had improved. Of course, that may have had more to do with Sean's cooking. She was an out-of-the-box kind of gal. At least Sean did admit he only knew how to cook five different things. All recipes his two sisters had given him.

Stepping back into the kitchen before they saw her, she quickly finished putting away the pantry items he'd used so that she could join them. Funny, at the beginning of dinner, her head had spun with thoughts of how to graciously get rid of him. Now she hoped the game wouldn't end soon.

She'd learned so much about him that she really liked. He enjoyed children. It was obvious by the way he spoke of them that he adored his nieces and nephews, but didn't see them as often as he liked, since their parents' military careers had them strewn across the country.

Still, she worried about Corey getting too attached. There'd be many nights when Sean would be busy or had a date and…

The thought was startlingly and inappropriately dismal. He was young, good-looking. Of course he'd have dates. Many dates. It didn't matter to her. Not in the least. And if it did, it damn well shouldn't.

After hanging up the dish towel, she took a last look around the kitchen, then ducked out to the kennel for a final check on her overnight guests. She came around the front of the house this time and saw his dark blue truck parked in the driveway.

So where was the red Corvette? Was Hannah right? Had he been trying to impress Alana? The thought annoyed her. What a juvenile stunt. It sounded like something Brad would do.

Except Sean was young and single, and if that's what he chose to spend his money on, so be it. It was his right. And she'd do well to remember his taste in expensive toys.

Just as she entered the family room, the game came to an end. She stood behind the couch and waited for the last strikeout and final score to be announced.

"Two back-to-back home runs." Sean lifted a hand and Corey gave him five. "Awesome."

"Awesome," Corey agreed around a yawn. He turned when he saw Alana out of the corner of his eye. "Hi, Mom, you missed a good game. The Mariners whooped the Yankees."

"I see that." She smiled. "But guess what?"

His gaze flew to the antique grandfather clock that her parents had given her right before the move to Seattle. "Aw, Mom, can't I stay up a little later?"

"It's already past your bedtime."

He looked to Sean for help.

"Come on, sport, do like your mom says." Sean tugged at Corey's ear. "I've got to go anyway. Tomorrow is an early work day for me."

Alana should have been glad she didn't have to get him to leave. She wasn't. She liked talking to him. It was probably the adult conversation that appealed. It had nothing to do with him personally.

Corey heaved a heavy put-upon sigh. "Okay, but will I see you tomorrow?"

"Maybe. Depends on how work goes."

Disappointment crossed Corey's face. "Okay." He pushed off the couch, and with a yawn, lumbered toward the hall. "Good night."

"Hey."

He looked back at Sean who put up a hand. Corey grinned and hurried back to high-five him.

Sean tugged on his ear. "Good night, kiddo."

"Don't forget to brush your teeth," Alana said. "I'll be in shortly to tuck you in and get my kiss."

"All right." He left a trail of reluctance all the way down the hall.

"Well…" Alana turned to Sean, clasping her hands together, nervous suddenly. "Thanks so much for fixing dinner. Everything was delicious. Even the wilted spinach salad."

"You sound surprised."

"I'm not a big fan of spinach."

"Ah, wait till you try my eggplant casserole."

Alana wrung her hands, struggling for the right words. The last thing she wanted to do was hurt his feelings.

"I know what you're thinking," he said with a smug nod. "But even people who hate eggplant like this dish. Of course, I don't usually tell them what's in it."

She gave him a wan smile. "It's not about egg-plant."

He stared at her for a moment. "I'm not going to like this, am I?"

She let out a self-conscious laugh. "Not a big deal, really. I just wanted—" Oh, God. "Would you like a cup of coffee? I can make some."

He smiled. "Go ahead, Alana. I'm a big boy. I can take it." He'd left the couch and stood close, too close, making her thoughts go haywire.

"I appreciate your interest in Corey. I really do. But I'm worried." She looked away, wishing the expression on his face wasn't so darn earnest. "I can't afford to let Corey become attached to you."

"Why?"

"Corey's never had an adult male friend. He misses his father and he might get confused when you aren't available to him."

"Friends generally aren't available twenty-four/seven."

"I understand, but we're talking about my son, and I don't want to see him hurt any more than he's already been."

"And if I promise not to hurt him?"

"You know you can't make that promise."

He studied her for a moment. "You're right. But I can promise not to deliberately do anything that would hurt him."

"Not good enough. He's too fragile."

"So you think he should be sheltered from society, from any possible hurt?"

"That would be impossible. And ridiculous." She started to add that she didn't appreciate his commentary on her parenting technique, but then thought better of it. Why get into it? In a minute he'd be gone. Out of their lives. And again it would be just her and Corey.

"I have a question," he said finally.

She raised her eyebrows and waited. He could ask. It didn't mean she had to answer.

"Do you think it's better for him to be isolated than to risk getting hurt?"

She folded her arms across her chest and answered with silence.

He stared at her a long moment. Long enough for her to realize they weren't talking only about Corey.

CHAPTER SIX

"I HEARD FROM Debbie North last night." Hannah absently flipped through the mail on her desk at the day care. The power bill she set aside, not anxious to ruin her day.

Alexandra glanced up from the newspaper. "She's back from the San Juan Islands already?"

"She only wanted a look at the things Mom is giving away. I told her she should stay overnight and make a vacation out of the trip, but she seemed in a frenzy about something."

"It's about the cross, of course. You know she thinks it's related to the theft at Our Lady of Mercy all those years ago. Did you ask your mom about it?"

Alexandra didn't say anything about the fire that had taken place the same night as the theft. The fire that burned down her house and killed both her parents. Hannah hated bringing it up. That's why she'd played dumb about Debbie's interest in the cross. It seemed as if the fire and the theft and Father Michael's murder were inseparable in most people's minds. Including Alexandra's.

"Mom barely remembered it." Hannah tore up a couple of advertisements and set aside two more bills.

"She thinks she may have picked it up on one of her buying trips for her business. Anyway, she doesn't see how it could have anything to do with Our Lady of Mercy."

"Hmm…"

Hannah looked up, her defenses rising. "What?"

Alexandra was grinning. "You know Debbie as well as I do. Once she smells a lead, there's no stopping her."

"Well, in this case, I'm afraid she's struck out," Hannah said, feeling foolish. She was touchy, she knew. First there had been the discrepancy in her blood type and her parents', and their insistence that it was the result of a lab mixup. Then she had come across her mother's love letters to Louis Kinard when she'd been at Olivia's island place. If her mother could lie about something like her daughter's paternity… Hannah ruthlessly pushed aside the thought. In her mind and in her heart, Kenneth Richards was the only father she would ever have. "I hope she at least found some pieces she can use in her apartment."

"Didn't she say?"

"I didn't talk to her. She left a message on my answering machine to meet her at Mickey's Roadhouse this evening at six."

Alexandra's gaze strayed toward the window. "Why so far away? That's way up in the mountains and the weather doesn't look good."

"I don't know." Hannah finished sorting the mail. "They have great onion rings there, though."

"Maybe, but I sure wouldn't go that far for them."

The door to the office opened, and Alana poked her head inside. "Hey, you two." She slipped inside and smoothed back her windblown hair. "Am I interrupting or are you goofing off?"

"Would it matter?" Alexandra motioned her closer. "Get in here and tell us about your date with Sean. Hannah said you wouldn't give her any details when you picked up Corey Sunday night."

"It wasn't a date."

Alexandra snorted, and Hannah grinned.

"Not really," Alana said, her cheeks turning pink. "I only went out with him to appease Corey."

"Okay, so how did this appeasement go?" Alexandra asked, laughing and ducking when Alana threw a crumpled piece of paper at her.

"I came here to pick up my son, not take abuse from you two."

"What?" Hannah widened her eyes. "I haven't said a word."

"You didn't have to." Alana frowned. "Everyone is making way too much of this."

"Do tell."

Alana sighed. "Sean is a very nice guy."

"And?"

"And that's it. I'm sure he comes around to see Corey more than he does me."

Hannah and Alexandra exchanged glances, and Hannah said, "He's been to your house since the date?"

Alana's cheeks got pinker. "To see Corey." She shrugged. "He made us dinner once." After a minute of silence, she added, "And last night he brought pizza." She looked from Hannah to Alexandra. "What?"

"So far all you've done is eat?" Alexandra asked, frowning.

Alana laughed. "You guys are too much. We're just friends, okay?"

"Good start." Alexandra pushed back her chair. "All kidding aside, Sean is good people. You should see when he gets back from visiting his nieces and nephews. Tons of pictures. And you can tell all the kids adore him. I bet he ends up with a brood of his own someday."

"I'm surprised he doesn't have a family already," Alana murmured half to herself.

"He's only twenty-nine," Hannah said. "He has time."

Alana's expression fell. "That's all, huh?"

"Twenty-nine is a problem?"

Alana blinked. "Of course not. He's just a friend."

Hannah bit back a laugh. At the same time, the office door opened. Her mother stood in the doorway, looking as regal as ever, her golden highlighted hair perfectly coiffed, the peach linen suit tailor made for her slim figure.

"Good afternoon, ladies," she said sweeping into the room with a critical glance at the mess of papers on Hannah's desk.

Hannah did her best to ignore the implied criticism. "Alana, have you met my mother?"

"Yes, briefly when I picked up Corey a couple of

weeks ago.'' Alana gave Olivia a polite smile. "Nice to see you again, Mrs. Richards." She nodded to Hannah and Alexandra. "I'd better go round up my son. See you later."

She left, and the room descended into silence. Not an unusual occurrence among Hannah's friends when her mother was around. When she was younger, it used to embarrass Hannah that her mother acted as if she were better than everyone else.

The truth was, her family had been no better off than Alexandra's or Katherine's. Their fathers were partners in the business they'd started together, social and financial equals, until the scandal...

Finally Alexandra asked, "What are you doing in this area of town, Olivia?"

One perfectly arched eyebrow rose. "Why shouldn't I come see my daughter?"

With a sigh, Alexandra got up. "It was just a question. You two go ahead and visit. I've got an errand to run."

Hannah watched her leave, saying nothing, even though she knew her friend didn't have anywhere in particular to go. Since Alexandra had returned to Seattle last fall, a tension had existed between Olivia and her, and Hannah didn't think either of them could say why.

"Alexandra?"

Reluctantly, Alexandra stopped at the door and turned toward Olivia.

"How's that homeless bum you've been helping? Devlin, I believe his name is. Any progress?"

"Mother, he's not a bum," Hannah cut in, not trying to hide her annoyance.

"Oh." Olivia sat on one of the guest chairs and looked from her daughter to Alexandra. "He's found a home and job then?"

Alexandra looked as if she wanted to bite Olivia's head off. She was very protective of the homeless man who'd been hanging around the day care almost since it opened. He was a sweet, gentle man who'd been kind to everyone at Forrester Square, yet had never asked for a thing. Alexandra was on a mission to help him.

"He's fine," she said tightly, and then to Hannah, "I'll see you later."

Hannah waited until the door was closed behind her before giving her mother the evil eye. "Why did you do that?"

"Do what?" She lifted her chin. "I was trying to make polite conversation."

Hannah shook her head with disgust, though she knew better than to pursue the topic. Instead, she gave herself a timeout by going across the room to get more coffee. She lifted her mug. "Want some?"

"Heavens, no." Her mother almost never drank coffee in the afternoon. "And you should watch how much you drink now that you're pregnant. Actually, I came by to see if you'd like to go for tea."

"Sorry. I can't."

"What's so pressing around here that you can't spend an hour with me?"

Hannah concentrated on pouring her coffee. Their

relationship would never be the same, she knew, not since she'd found out her mother had lied about her paternity all these years. But Olivia was still her mother.

Sighing, she turned around. "I really can't. I'm meeting Debbie North this evening."

"Oh, is she back from the island?"

"Apparently, she got in last night."

Looking bored, Olivia studied her manicure. "Did she find anything she wants for her apartment?"

"I don't know. Guess she'll tell me when I see her later."

Olivia stood abruptly. "All right, I suppose I'll go have tea by myself."

"Another time, okay, Mom?"

"Of course, dear." She smiled and kissed Hannah's cheek. "Let's make it soon. Have fun with Debbie."

Over the rim of her cup, Hannah watched her leave the office. Olivia Richards was a difficult woman to figure out. Sometimes she was warm and maternal, and other times she was so cool and calculating, Hannah felt as if she didn't know her at all.

"WHAT ARE YOU DOING?" Alana stared at Sean's jean-clad legs. She could only see him from the waist down. Not that the view was so awful. In fact, it was damn fine.

He'd come over about half an hour ago while she was bandaging the hind leg of the O'Rourkes' poodle after the poor little guy tangled with a wire fence. Corey had promptly come to the clinic and told her

Sean was at the house. But what the heck was he doing with his head stuck under her kitchen sink?

The way he wiggled his hips to work his way out from under the sink made her tummy flutter. He ducked his head to the side and smiled at her. "Hello, Alana."

Her gaze strayed to the tool belt lying beside him. "You're fixing that drip, aren't you?"

He frowned. "You knew about it?"

"Well, yes."

"And you didn't have it fixed?"

"I didn't want to call a plumber. I thought maybe I could manage it myself."

He made a face. "How long has it been leaking?"

"I wouldn't go so far as to say that it's a leak. A small drip, really."

Sean chuckled. "Well, it doesn't matter now. It's fixed."

"Really?"

"The drain trap had rusted through. I replaced it, so that should take care of it."

"Thank you. Of course I'll pay you."

His expression darkened. "Give me a break," he said, and ducked back under the sink.

Alana hadn't meant to offend him. "Can I help?"

"Nope. I just have to tighten this—" He grunted. "Got it." He slid out again, and this time raised himself to a sitting position. His hair was as unruly as ever, and he couldn't seem to keep it out of his face. With his fingers, he combed it back off his forehead.

Alana giggled.

"What?"

"You have a streak of something right there." She pointed to his cheek.

"Here?" He touched a spot near his ear.

"No, a little higher."

"Here?" She shook her head. "I'll get you a mirror."

"Just wipe it off for me."

She sucked in a breath. The idea of touching him sent a shiver of excitement up her spine. She was being silly, of course, but goodness...

Crouching closer to him, she used the pad of her thumb to wipe the smear. "I think I made it worse."

He closed his hand over hers. "I doubt it," he said, his voice lowered.

She swallowed. "Where's Corey?"

"In his room."

When she struggled to rise, he held her hand firmly. "He's supposed to be cleaning his room. I need to go check on him."

"He's fine, Alana."

"I'll just—"

"Don't run away."

"I'm not." She'd never been this close to him before, not close enough to see how his eyes went from green to golden. Or close enough to smell his clean pine scent. She swallowed, wanting to move still closer, yet at the same time wanting to get as far away as possible. "It's important that he cleans his room before dinner. It's one of his chores."

The corners of Sean's lips curved upward. "Then he'll be busy awhile, won't he?"

Alana tried to get up again but nearly lost her balance. "Sean, we can't—"

"Can't what?"

She had to grasp his shoulders to keep from falling backward, then briefly touched her lips to his. "Do this."

The shock in his eyes reflected her own. Was she crazy? Was she that deprived?

"You're right, we shouldn't do this," he said with a seriousness that made her want to run and hide in shame. "This would be much better."

He cupped the back of her head with one hand and claimed her lips with his. She started to retreat, but he opened his mouth and teased her lips apart with the tip of his tongue.

Heat filled her belly and spread up to her chest. She wanted to dive inside of him, lose herself for an hour or two. But Corey could...

She pulled away and struggled to her feet. "I'm sorry," she murmured, tucking some loose hair back into her ponytail. "I shouldn't have done that. This is my fault."

Sean didn't move, but only stared up at her. "Why should this be anyone's *fault*? It was bound to happen."

"Why? I thought I made it clear you were welcome here to visit Corey. But as far as anything between us—"

He smiled in a patronizing way that made her want

to smack him. It also made her feel like a jackass. She was the moron who'd initiated the kiss.

She sighed. She'd apologize one more time, make it clear that there could be no romantic involvement between them, and then finito, the end.

"Mom, what should I do with this?"

The sound of Corey's voice sobered her quickly. She turned to see what he was referring to. He held up the pole he'd used when they'd gone fishing three weeks ago.

"Honey, have you had that in your room all this time?"

He shrugged. "In my closet."

"You know it belongs in the garage with the other poles."

With a mutinous lift of his chin, he said, "I knew where it belonged in our old house."

Alana gritted her teeth. She would not let him make her feel guilty for the move. She'd done it for him, after all. "Well, now that you know where it belongs here, please, go put it away."

"I'll do it later." He rested the pole against the wall. "I wanna help Sean."

"Corey, it will only take you a minute."

At her don't-argue-with-me tone, he grabbed the pole, and with a pouting lower lip, slipped out the back door.

She heard Sean chuckle. "What?"

He quickly lost the grin and saluted her. "Nothing, Captain Fletcher. Permission to stand, ma'am."

"Very funny."

He got to his feet. "You like to fish, too? Or do you go mostly for Corey?"

The familiar way he touched her arm alarmed her. She shifted nervously. "I like the outdoors. Fishing, hiking, waterskiing, you name it."

"No kidding." A pleased grin spread across his face. "Me, too. What are you doing this Saturday?"

"Working."

"All day?" He picked up the wrench and pliers he'd been using, and neatly returned them to their slots in the small toolbox.

"Yup."

"What about Sunday?"

She hesitated. How could they spend a day together after what had just happened?

As if he could read her mind, he said, "Corey will be there to chaperone."

Alana snorted. "Corey is going to be grounded if he doesn't keep his room straight and put fishing poles where they belong."

"You're not serious." Sean set his toolbox aside and stared at her.

Okay, so she'd exaggerated. She wouldn't ground him for anything that trivial. But the way Sean looked at her made her want to stand her ground. Show him that she took her responsibility as a parent seriously and wouldn't tolerate any interference. And worse, his expression reminded her of Brad when he thought she was being too hard on Corey.

"He's just a kid," Sean continued. "He'll have enough time in life for rules and regulations."

"How he prepares for that life is by learning to obey rules in childhood."

"Yes, Captain."

"Quit calling me that. You don't have kids. You don't understand."

"You're right. I don't understand." Sean shook his head. He hadn't figured Alana to be such a strict disciplinarian. "But not because I don't have kids. I know enough that you gotta let a kid be a kid. Hell, he'll be burdened with enough responsibilities later."

"Conducting oneself like an adult is not necessarily a burden."

"Don't split hairs. You know what I mean." He heaved a heavy sigh, sorry as hell he'd gotten into this conversation. His father, the captain, had been strict. Too strict, and Sean had resented him for not being able to tell the difference between his own son and a recruit.

Of course Alana wasn't nearly as bad. She obviously had a real soft spot for Corey, and seemed to make him her priority. That was one of the things he really liked about her. "Look, Alana, he already feels it's his responsibility to make you happy. Doesn't that tell you something?"

A stricken look drained the color from her face. "Because he wanted to auction me off?"

"That, and how he keeps pushing us together. Most kids of divorced parents get jealous if another person enters their lives."

She drew in her lower lip for a pregnant moment. "I'm strict because he needs guidelines. His father doesn't care what Corey does, and maybe I overcompensate. I certainly don't mean to be unreasonable.''

"Hey.'' He touched her arm. She didn't flinch or pull away. Good sign. "I don't mean to give you a hard time. Corey said something about being the man of the house now, and I guess it pushed a button. He's not a man, he's still a boy.''

She did flinch then, and turned toward the refrigerator. "Would you like something to drink? Some lemonade or iced tea? I think I might even have another beer left.''

Her tone was crisp, formal. Damn, he wished he'd kept his mouth shut. Who the hell did he think he was to offer his opinion?

"Hey, Sean, is there another game on TV tonight?'' Corey had come barreling through the door, his face flushed from running. "We could watch it together.''

Sean's gaze locked with Alana's. She obviously still wasn't happy with him. "Another time, okay, sport. I was out late last night. I gotta go home and get some shut-eye.''

The lie pricked him like a needle. He turned away from the disappointment in Corey's eyes and picked up his toolbox. A thought occurred to him and he tried not to smile, knowing he was probably about to get himself in bigger trouble. Tough.

"Corey, I asked your mom if you two would like to go fishing this weekend,'' he said, sliding her a glance, and getting a look that could melt steel. "Talk her into it, would you?''

CHAPTER SEVEN

"WHY DO YOU SUPPOSE Katherine didn't want anyone to pick her up at the airport?" Hannah asked, frowning at the wall clock. "She should have been here by now."

Alexandra made a face. "Quit being paranoid because you got stood up last night."

"Paranoid? You don't think it was odd for Debbie not to show? I called her at home at least three times and got her answering machine. Her cell phone sent me directly to voice mail. Weird. On the message she left me, she sounded so excited to talk. I don't get it."

"She probably had an article to write or got sent on a last-minute assignment."

Hannah shook her head. "She would have called."

"Here." Alexandra tossed the morning's newspaper onto Hannah's desk. "Read this. Get your mind off Katherine. She'll be here soon."

Hannah wandered down to the day care kitchen and made herself a cup of coffee—decaf this time. Was it a full moon, or what? Katherine had sounded so cryptic about her return from Alaska, and it wasn't at all like Debbie not to keep their date or call otherwise.

Odd. She brought her mug back to her desk and

then flipped through her Rolodex. She should know Debbie's number by heart by now. She punched in her home number, got her answering machine, and then tried her cell. No luck.

Idly she leafed through the newspaper. If she hadn't heard from Debbie by the end of the day, she'd call the paper. In fact, just to assure herself, she decided to call now. Debbie would answer the phone, offer her apology, and Hannah could quit worrying.

Before she punched in the first number, an article on the second page caught her eye. She replaced the receiver and picked up the newspaper, staring at the headlines.

Her stomach rolled. Bile rose in her throat.

One Of Our Own Killed, it read.

Debbie North had apparently run off the road. Her car had flipped over into a ditch. She was found dead by a passing motorist. Police were investigating whether foul play was involved.

Hannah put a hand to her mouth, not trusting that she wouldn't lose her breakfast. This couldn't be happening.

"Hannah? What's wrong?" Alexandra got up from her desk and came to stand beside her. She touched her shoulder. "Hannah?"

Unable to speak, Hannah pointed at the paper lying on her desk. She wrapped her other arm around herself.

Alexandra scanned the paper, letting out a shriek when she came to the article. "Oh, my God. Oh, my God."

Hannah shook her head in denial, tears filling her eyes. This couldn't be possible.

As she sank into a chair, Alexandra continued to stare at the article. "I don't believe this."

Hannah still couldn't speak. She'd known something was wrong. She'd felt it deep in her gut. Why hadn't she kept calling Debbie, or suggested they meet someplace closer, or… Oh, God, she didn't know what to think, didn't know what she could've done to make things different.

"Hannah?" She looked into her friend's grief-stricken eyes.

"I know what you're doing, Hannah." Alexandra leaned over and clasped her hands around Hannah's. "It was an unfortunate accident. Nothing you could have changed."

"But it was foggy and drizzly and I should have told her we should meet here, or her place, or anywhere closer."

"Hannah…don't. I liked Debbie and I'm sorry this happened, but you can't make yourself sick over it. You've got the baby to think of…"

Nodding, she sniffed, grabbed a tissue and dabbed at her eyes and nose. "I need to call Jack."

"Good idea." Alexandra squeezed her hand before letting it go. "That'll make you feel better."

No sarcasm tainted her words. Obviously there was nothing Jack could do, but Hannah knew she'd find comfort in her husband's voice, reassurance in his quiet strength.

She picked up the receiver, her heart heavy with

grief. For the sake of her sanity, Hannah wished she could shake the feeling that Debbie's death was somehow her fault.

SOMETHING WAS different about Katherine. Hannah and Alexandra both noticed it immediately. That didn't mean either one of them was prepared for the bomb she dropped.

"I can't believe you're married." Alexandra shook her head. "I mean, I knew going to Alaska was kind of a trial run, but good grief. You—you're married." Katherine laughed.

"Ain't it grand?"

"Well, yes, it's terrific."

Hannah and Katherine exchanged glances. Obviously Katherine had heard the same wistfulness in their friend's voice that Hannah heard. No wonder. They'd both gotten married in a short period of time. Alexandra had to be feeling a bit at loose ends.

"Well, now, Alexandra, it's not as if anything is going to change," Hannah said, putting an arm around her shoulder. "I'm still here, aren't I?"

She smiled at Katherine. Only Katherine didn't smile back. In fact, she winced. Alexandra caught the reaction, too. They both stared at Katherine, waiting for her to say something.

Briefly she closed her eyes, and then cleared her throat. "I really hate delivering this news, especially with what you just told me about Debbie and all, but there's no way around it."

"Go ahead," Alexandra said when Katherine hesitated too long.

"I'm moving to Alaska."

"What!" Alexandra's eyes widened. She abruptly looked at Hannah. "Did you know about this?"

"Of course not." Although Hannah realized she shouldn't be surprised, considering Nick was a bush pilot. But everything had happened so fast.

"I know you're both disappointed." Sighing, Katherine sank into her office chair and reluctantly met her friends' eyes. "God, this is even harder than I thought it would be. Nick's a bush pilot. His life and job are in Alaska. It makes sense for me to move there." A smile flitted across her lips. "I have to tell you—I fell in love with Nick and his three adorable little girls, but I also fell hopelessly in love with Alaska."

It had been one hell of a day, Hannah thought. She didn't think she could say anything halfway intelligent.

"You know I love you guys," Katherine said, her eyes getting glassy.

"And we love you." Hannah swallowed around the lump in her throat. "We're happy for you. Truly." She looked to Alexandra for support. She nodded on cue. "It's just a surprise. That's all."

"I know. Maybe I should have called from Alaska and not waited until I got back."

"It wouldn't have mattered." Hannah got up from her chair to give Katherine a hug. "We'll miss you, of course, but you're happy. That's all that matters."

Alexandra got up to join them in a group hug. "Yeah, go ahead and ditch us for some guy."

Katherine laughed. "Ah, Alexandra, I've really treasured these past months since you've been back."

"Me, too." Alexandra sniffed.

"Alaska isn't that far from Seattle, and Nick says he'll fly me down here any time I want. I'll see both of you often. I promise."

"We'll hold you to that." Hannah smiled. "Anyway, we'll have to talk to you about day-care business. That has to mean phone calls twice a week, right?"

Katherine's expression clouded. "That's something else we need to discuss." She looked miserable suddenly, and Hannah's chest tightened. "I want to sell my share of Forrester Square."

"WANT ANOTHER LATTE?" Alexandra asked as she pushed back from the table. "I'm buying."

Hannah shook her head. If she had one more sip of anything, she'd explode.

Caffeine Hy's had been jam-packed when she and Alexandra had gotten there after the day care closed, four hours ago. The coffeehouse had since emptied out, then filled up with the after-theater crowd, and was now deserted again. Except for Maddy Lagerfeldt, who worked at the local library and offered a story program for the preschool children at the day care. She'd been drinking tea and reading for the past couple of hours, only looking up when someone came in the door.

Alexandra came back with another large-size latte

and sat down. "Tell me you had an absolutely brilliant idea while I was gone."

"Right." Hannah was so exhausted she could barely sit up straight. "It's ironic that we worked our butts off to put on the auction so that we wouldn't have to sell the day care, and now..." She shook her head in total dismay.

"So you're leaning toward selling," Alexandra said, pushing her mug aside.

"I'm not sure we have any other options. Neither one of us wants the responsibility of running the show."

Alexandra's gaze strayed out the window at the passing car lights. Traffic had died down. No wonder. It was late. They should both have gone home by now. "Katherine pretty much directed everything." She sighed. "Apart from you and me handling the accounting, we've been more like the gofers."

Hannah nodded. "Nothing wrong with that, since that's the way we all wanted it. But with my new family and all..."

"Hey, I don't blame you. I don't have anything tying me down and I still don't want the responsibility." Alexandra shrugged. "I don't blame Katherine, either. She's obviously very happy. But the day care was her dream, and if we have to sell, then so be it."

The door opened, letting in some street noise, and they both looked to see who'd come in.

The woman was in her midfifties, very well dressed, her hairstyle short and sensible. She carried a large leather portfolio, the type that might hold artwork. She looked vaguely familiar.

"Lisa, I'm glad you made it." Maddy Lagerfeldt closed her book and put it down. "I was starting to worry."

"I apologize. My plane was late." The woman smiled at Hannah and Alexandra before taking a seat at Maddy's table. "And then it was so foggy we couldn't land for over half an hour."

"Good old Seattle." Maddy grinned. "I'll get your drink. What would you like?"

The woman asked for plain black coffee, and Maddy went up to the counter for it.

Alexandra looked over her shoulder. "Maddy, I think Alice went to the bathroom. She won't care if you pour your own."

Maddy sighed and slipped behind the counter. "She's probably hiding in the back, talking on her cell phone."

The other woman laughed. "Sounds like you all are regulars."

"Too regular, sometimes," Alexandra confessed.

"That's nice, though. I'm from back east, and I'm sure there are places like this in the suburbs where everyone knows everyone else, but not where I live." Her friendly smile went from Alexandra to Hannah. "I remember you. You work at Forrester Square Day Care. One of the owners, right?"

Hannah remembered now. She'd met the woman briefly after the auction "You're Lisa DeWitt."

"Yes, that's right. I picked up some art the Gray Gallery had donated."

"You don't live here, though?"

Maddy returned with two coffees.

"Thanks, you're a doll," Lisa said, accepting the cup and immediately taking a sip. "I'm actually on vacation, but I had to take a day trip to San Francisco to pick up an art piece for my old alma mater."

"Hannah..." Maddy reclaimed her seat. "Lisa went to Smith. Didn't your mother go there, too?"

"Yes." Hannah studied Lisa for a moment. "She's probably about your age." She grimaced. "And then again, you might be younger and I'll have egg on my face."

Lisa laughed softly. "Tell you what, if she graduated in the midsixties, I'll know her. It's a small school and we alumni are a tight group. What's her name?"

"Well, at the time it was Brawney. Olivia Brawney."

Lisa frowned. "No, the name doesn't sound familiar at all."

Hannah thought for a moment. "I believe she graduated in either sixty-five or sixty-six."

"I was there until sixty-six." Lisa's frown deepened. "I knew all the girls, but that name just doesn't ring a bell. Does she have any distinguishing features?"

"Not really." Hannah shrugged. "It doesn't matter. But I will mention your name to her."

The door opened again, diverting everyone's attention. When Hannah looked back at Alexandra, she had the most peculiar look on her face. One that made Hannah uneasy.

IT HAD BEEN FOUR DAYS and not a word from Sean. Alana put water on to boil for tea and stared at the telephone. She should call him. Not for her sake, but for Corey's. It wasn't his fault that she'd been rude to Sean, that she had blasted him about not understanding the role of a parent. Obviously she'd hurt his feelings. That was the reason he was staying away.

She closed her eyes and pinched the bridge of her nose, trying to decide if she should call or not. He might get the wrong idea, even if she did explain it was for Corey's benefit.

Darn it.

She picked up the phone before she lost her nerve, started to punch in the area code and realized she didn't know his number. She'd never called him. He'd always called them.

Of course she could probably get it from the phone book or from Hannah. Oh, God, that wouldn't do. Hannah would get the wrong idea.

Corey popped his head in the kitchen. He'd been playing with the dogs in the backyard and his shirt was covered in grass stains. "Did Sean call today?"

"No. Wash your hands, young man, before you touch any food."

He'd made it to the refrigerator. Groaning, he went to the sink and stepped up on the stool she now kept there so that he could reach the faucet. "He said he wanted to go fishing. Why hasn't he called?"

"I don't know, honey." The kettle whistled, signaling the water was ready for her tea. She chose some soothing chamomile and then poured the boiling water into a mug.

"Can we call him?"

"I don't know his number."

His hands washed, Corey went to the refrigerator and opened the door. He had the same annoying habit as his father—standing with the refrigerator door open forever while he studied the contents he probably knew by heart.

"Have an apple. You haven't had any fruit today yet."

He made a face, but reached for a Granny Smith. "I wanna call Sean."

Alana closed the fridge door. "I'll look in the phone book to see if he's listed. Otherwise, we'll just have to wait until we hear from him."

She leafed through the white pages, half expecting him not to be listed. Not only did she find his name immediately, but a business number was listed as well, for Everett Construction. Was it a family business, she wondered? Sean seemed too young to have started his own company.

"Mom…" Corey drawled out her name in that whiny voice that drove her crazy. "Did you find it?"

"Yes, now hush while I call." She punched in the numbers and briefly considered letting Corey speak to him. But that would be childish. Anyway, Sean would know she'd have to have found his number.

After the third ring, a woman answered. She sounded young. Really young.

Alana almost hung up. She cleared her throat. "May I speak with Sean Everett, please?"

She heard a sound like gum popping, and then, "Who's calling?"

"Alana Fletcher."

"You a friend of his?"

Good question. Using the term loosely, she supposed so. "Uh, yes."

"Are you one of his customers?" the girl asked.

Alana was pretty sure she was young enough to be considered a girl, certainly a teenager. The thought made her a little sick. Which was foolish. She'd already acknowledged that Sean was too young for her.

"No, I'm, well, actually he's a friend of my son Corey, and we—"

"Oh, you're Corey's mom. Cool."

Alana frowned. "You've met my son?"

"No, but Sean talks about him. And you."

"Oh."

"Look, I, uh…" The girl hesitated. "I'm not supposed to tell just anybody this, or my mom would kill me, but being as I sort of know you—" She paused again. "Sean had an accident and he's in the hospital."

The floor seemed to shift beneath Alana's feet. "Is he okay?"

"I think so. He's been there for three days, but my mom says he should be released soon."

"Was it a car accident?"

"Nope. Something happened at work. I gotta go

now. I just came over to feed his dog and water his plants.''

"Wait! Can you tell me which hospital he's in?''

"Um, I'm not sure. Probably Seattle Memorial. My mom would know.''

"That's all right. Thank you.'' Alana hung up, her mind still reeling.

Seattle Memorial was the logical hospital. It was the largest and the closest. But darn it, why hadn't she at least gotten the girl's name and number, just in case...

"What's wrong, Mom?'' Corey stared up at her, his eyes round and concerned. "Did something happen to Sean?''

"I'm not sure, honey.'' She stroked his hair for a moment, not wanting to alarm him. "But I'm going to find out.''

She grabbed the phone book and found the hospital's number. She gave his name and they immediately patched her through to his room. It rang a long time and then a woman answered.

"Room two-two-seven,'' she said in a crisp, no-nonsense tone. Had to be a nurse.

"Is this Sean Everett's room?''

"Yes, but he's unable to come to the phone.''

Alana's pulse skidded. The nurse hadn't said "for the moment,'' only that he was *unable*. She took a deep breath. "Is he able to have visitors?''

The woman hesitated. "Are you family?''

She looked down into Corey's anxious face. She had to find out something. "This is Dr. Alana Fletcher. I'm a friend of Sean's.''

"Oh, Dr. Fletcher, I'm sure it would be fine if you

came to see him.'' The woman's entire tone changed. If she only knew Alana was a vet and not an M.D.

"With whom am I speaking?"

"Emma Tompkins, his nurse."

"I'll be there within the hour, Emma, but can you give me a brief prognosis?"

"Well, Mr. Everett suffered a head injury…"

Alana gasped. "A head injury?"

"Yes, but nothing serious," the nurse added quickly.

Right. "Then why hasn't he been released?" Alana knew darn well hospitals and insurance companies were both anxious to get rid of patients as soon as possible.

After a brief hesitation, long enough for Alana's stomach to tie up in knots, Emma Tompkins said, "Perhaps you should speak with his doctor."

She didn't like the sound of that. Corey tugged at her hand and she pulled herself together enough to give him an encouraging smile.

Damn that Sean. Had he been out late the night before the accident at some bar watching a ball game or trying to pick up a woman? The last time they'd seen him he'd admitted he'd been out too late the previous night. Had fatigue caused the accident?

It didn't matter right now and she'd do well not to think about it. She glanced at her watch. "Thank you, Ms. Tompkins. I'll be there in twenty minutes."

CHAPTER EIGHT

"AMNESIA?" ALANA STARED at Emma Tompkins. "Amnesia?" It sounded so...impossible.

"The doctor called a few minutes after we'd hung up and he was pleased you were coming to see Mr. Everett. Dr. Lerner is hoping that seeing you will help jog his memory."

"So this isn't anything serious or permanent?"

"Well, as you know, Dr. Fletcher, amnesia is difficult to predict. The condition could last a day, a month, or sometimes there is no recovery."

Alana swallowed, her gaze straying past the nurse to Sean, who was lying in the hospital bed, his eyes closed, his complexion pale beneath the bandage wrapped around his head.

Emma touched her arm and Alana looked back at her to see compassion in her pale blue eyes. "It's hard to be professional and detached when the patient is someone we care about personally. Dr. Lerner feels quite certain the memory loss will pass within a week."

"Thanks." Her gaze went back to Sean. "I don't want to wake him."

"He probably isn't asleep, but even so, it's best that he see a face he may recognize."

Alana hesitated. Corey waited in the lobby with a hospital volunteer. "I think I'll go speak with my son first. He's too young to come in, but I just want to reassure him."

"Does he know Mr. Everett?"

"Actually, he's Sean's friend."

The woman's graying eyebrows rose. "Tell you what, maybe it would be helpful if your son came in for a brief visit. Who knows? Perhaps Mr. Everett will recognize him."

"I suppose." But did she really want to expose Corey to this? She glanced at Sean. He'd opened his eyes.

"Why don't you go in and see if he recognizes you, while I go get your son?"

Alana nodded. "His name is Corey." The woman turned to leave and Alana quickly added, "Please, stay with him outside the room and I'll come out for him."

"I understand." Her smile was kind and Alana felt a tad guilty for allowing her to believe she was a medical doctor.

Sean stared at the ceiling, his expression intense. He turned his head toward Alana when she got closer to the bed. No sign of recognition. In fact, his brow furrowed as if he were struggling to identify her.

"Hi, Sean," she said softly. "Heard you're not feeling too well. What happened?"

He slowly shook his head. "I don't remember."

Her heart thudded. He didn't even look the same without his ever-present smile. She moved a little closer but resisted the urge to take his hand. "Do you know who I am?"

Again, he shook his head, yet carefully studied her face. His gaze traveled down to her breasts and lingered, before falling to her waist and hips. "I should know you," he whispered.

"It's okay," she said, lightly stroking the top of his hand. "You will. Give it time."

He stared at her hand and then turned his over so that their palms met. He slipped his fingers between hers, and his grip tightened. "You feel right."

Alana hesitated. She didn't want to jerk away, but neither did she want to foster the wrong idea.

Emma Tompkins saved her from making a decision when she called from the doorway. Alana could see Corey's arm, but Emma blocked his way inside.

"I'll be right back, okay?" She wiggled her fingers a little, but it didn't seem as if he wanted to release her.

"Where are you going?"

"To bring a friend of yours in to see you."

"Wait."

Alana turned to him. His eyebrows dipped in frustration, and panic flitted across his face, making her heart ache. He looked so vulnerable she wanted to hug him. "Yes?"

"What's your name?"

She swallowed. "Alana."

His lips lifted a little. "Pretty name."

She gave him the best smile she could, considering she wanted to cry. "I'll be right back. I promise."

He nodded, and she hurried to the door. Ms. Tompkins and Corey stood just a few feet outside.

"I wanna see Sean, Mom," Corey said as soon as he saw her. "*She* won't let me." He threw Nurse Tompkins a dirty look.

"Corey." Alana glared at him.

"It's okay." The nurse waved a dismissive hand. "He's worried about his friend."

Still, it was no excuse to be rude, and Corey knew it. Alana looked into his concerned eyes and softened. She leaned down until she could meet his gaze. "Honey, Sean hurt his head during an accident at work. He has a bandage on, so he can heal properly. Understand?"

Corey nodded solemnly. "Just like when you have to bandage Coco when she gets tangled with those thorns."

"That's right." She gave him a reassuring smile. He spent a lot of time at the clinic with her, and saw wounded animals come in to be treated. "There's one other thing—Sean bumped his head really hard. It caused him to forget a lot of things. He'll remember more each day, but he might not know who you are right now."

Corey stared at her, his tiny eyebrows knitted together. "He'll remember me."

She shook her head. "He probably won't. Not because he doesn't want to, but because of the injury. But we can't push him. We have to give him time to heal and remember by himself, okay?"

He frowned, obviously not liking the situation, but nodded his understanding. "Can I see him now?"

"Yes, but you have to be very quiet and not get him excited." Alana rose and took his hand. "Ready?"

He nodded jerkily.

"I'll be right out here if you need me." The nurse patted Alana's arm and gently touched Corey's head.

As they walked into the room, Corey squeezed Alana's hand.

Sean wasn't asleep. His eyes were wide open and trained on the door. She didn't think he could've heard what they said. He'd simply known they were out there and had been waiting for them.

She felt Corey's hand start to pull away and she held on firmly so he wouldn't run and startle Sean.

Corey gave him one of his big toothy grins. "Hi, Sean."

Sean blinked. "Hi."

"You banged your head, huh?" Corey stood beside the bed and stared at the stark white bandage.

"Yeah, I guess I did." Sean touched his head and probed the edges of the bandage.

"How did you do that?"

Pain crossed Sean's face and he looked helplessly at Alana. "I don't know."

She tugged on Corey's hand. "Not too many questions, okay?"

Corey made a face, but nodded, and then promptly asked, "Do you remember me?"

A grin tugged at Sean's mouth. "Sorry, sport, I don't."

"Hey, you call me that all the time."

Hope sparked in Sean's hazel eyes and he shifted his narrowed gaze from Corey to Alana, as if straining to remember.

"My name is Corey, though. But you can call me whatever you want."

"Okay," Sean said slowly. "Corey."

Corey grinned up at Alana. "See? He remembers."

A laugh escaped Alana, and Sean stared at her, the searching look he gave her making her shiver.

The nurse poked her head in. "Sorry, folks, but I'll have to ask you to step out for a few minutes. We need to take his blood pressure and some other good stuff."

"Of course." Alana placed her hands on Corey's shoulders to steer him to the corridor.

"Hey, Sean, we'll be right back, okay?"

He nodded, and looked at Alana.

"Would you like us to come back?" she whispered.

"Yes."

"Okay."

He reached out and touched her arm. She stopped and he ran his palm up as far as he could, his gaze locked on hers.

A young woman in a white lab coat walked in carrying a tray of tubes and needles. "I won't be long and y'all can come back in to visit," she said as she slid on disposable gloves.

Alana sent Sean a sidelong glance and then hurried Corey out into the corridor.

Emma Tompkins pulled the door until it was ajar. "He doesn't seem to remember you, does he?"

"I don't think so."

"He remembered me. He called me Corey."

Alana and the nurse exchanged smiles.

"When can he go home?" Corey asked.

"Well, that's not an easy question to answer." The nurse glanced at the chart she was holding before returning it to the wall jacket. "Physically he's ready for release. We can't do anything for the amnesia. Time will take care of that."

Corey looked up at Alana with a wrinkled nose. "Huh?"

She smiled. "It means his memory can come back slowly in bits and pieces, or by tomorrow morning he may wake up and remember everything."

"So why does he have to stay here?" Corey hunched his shoulders. "It's creepy."

"Actually, it's better if he does go home—be around places and things and people who could trigger—" Emma smiled at Corey's confused expression. "Help him remember. But since he lives alone, according to his neighbor—" she glanced at Alana for confirmation she couldn't give "—we can't very well send him home with no one there to help him."

"He could come home with us." Corey's eyes lit up. "I could stay home from day care and—"

"Corey." Alana tugged at his shirtsleeve. "He can't."

"Why not?"

"Because he needs more help than you can give him."

"But *you're* there."

"I'm working."

"Yeah, but you come to the house a lot."

"Honey…" Alana looked at the nurse. "I have a clinic attached to the house."

Emma's eyebrows shot up in surprise.

"I'm a veterinarian," Alana explained.

"I thought you were a people doctor."

Alana looked away, embarrassed, because she'd darn well fostered that impression.

It didn't seem to matter to the nurse. "Anyway, Mr. Everett wouldn't really require as much care as you might think. He can be quite self-sufficient, but he may get confused or frightened, and that's when it's important someone is there to explain or allay his fears."

Corey tugged on Alana's hand. "Does that mean he can come home with us?"

"I'll have to think about it, honey. I—"

The lab technician came out of the room. "He's all yours."

Corey let go of Alana's hand and dashed back in before she could stop him.

"Sean!" He yelled far too loudly. "You're coming home with us."

TWO DAYS OUT OF THE hospital and Sean still couldn't remember a damn thing. Not quite true. He did recall that he lived in Seattle and that he worked in construction, but he couldn't remember specifically where he lived or even that his name was really Sean Everett. He had to trust that he was being told the truth. The whole thing sucked.

Of course Alana was another story. He completely trusted her. Even though he had no specific memory, he felt their closeness, knew for certain they had some kind of connection. He wondered if they'd been dating before the accident.

She'd only said that they were friends, but he had a feeling she was holding something back. The intimate way she looked at him when she thought he didn't notice made his body respond in a manner that went beyond friendship. Her presence soothed him. When she was at the clinic, he was restless, his mind reeling with frustration and despair.

And Corey... Great kid. Always trying to be helpful. Sometimes too chatty, but Sean probably needed the noise. Otherwise, he thought too hard, and gave himself gigantic headaches.

"Sean, I'm home." Corey's voice rang from the kitchen, where he normally dumped his backpack when he got home from day care.

Another three seconds and his excited, flushed face appeared in the den. "What are you reading?" he asked as he planted himself on the couch beside Sean.

"Books on home improvement and carpentry. Did you have a good day at school?"

"Sure. What's carpentry?"

"Building things."

"You already know how to do that."

The innocent statement was like a blow to the gut. Sean had been told he owned his own construction company, and that he was a carpenter and a mason. But damn, he couldn't remember any of it.

"Mom says we're having an early dinner because she has to go someplace tonight."

Sean's heart sank. The highlight of his day was spending time with Alana in the evening. Besides, he hated seeing her work all day and then having to cook and rush out again. "Hey, Corey, do you suppose I know how to cook?"

He nodded vigorously. "Better than Mom," he whispered, quickly checking over his shoulder.

Chuckling, Sean got to his feet. "We'll keep that our little secret." A sudden thought froze him to the spot. He already knew he'd fixed things around the house, that they were supposed to go fishing the Sunday after he'd had the accident. If he'd cooked for them, too...

He raked a hand through his hair, debating whether he should pump Corey for information. The kid talked a lot but didn't volunteer much...almost as if he'd been told not to. Sean cleared his throat. "So, I used to cook for you a lot, huh?"

Corey shrugged. "Sort of a lot."

"Was I around here much?"

Corey just stared at him with a slight frown.

"You know, kind of like I was your mom's boyfriend or something."

Corey blinked. An odd look crossed his face, and you could tell he was concentrating hard. Excitement sparkled in his eyes. You could almost see the wheels turning.

Sean ruffled his hair. "Hey, sport, what's going on?"

For a moment Corey was silent, then he flashed Sean a mischievous grin. "I'm not supposed to tell," he said, and pretended he was zipping his lips.

"Ah, I see." Seam made a show of thoughtfully scratching his jaw. "Well, now, I wouldn't want you to break any promises."

"I didn't promise nothing."

"But you aren't supposed to tell?"

Corey shrugged. "I just can't let Mom know I told."

Sean hid a smile. He really shouldn't be a party to this… "I won't tell her if you won't."

Corey peeked behind him and then tugged at Sean's hand. Sean crouched down so that Corey could get close to his ear. "You aren't her boyfriend," he whispered excitedly. "You guys are married."

ALANA SMELLED THE AROMA of baked chicken as soon as she opened the front door. Her stomach rumbled. She'd skipped lunch and was so tired she was afraid to sit down for fear she wouldn't be able to get up again.

She stopped at the kitchen door and silently watched Sean mash potatoes. Corey stood on the stool beside him, washing tomatoes. Sean bent his leg back, and with his foot, tapped Corey's rear end.

Corey immediately turned around to see who it was. "Hey, was that you?"

"What?"

"You know what." Corey flicked his wet hand at Sean.

Sean jumped back, but not quickly enough. Using his forearm, he wiped his face. "Okay, sport, this is war."

Corey giggled. "You started it."

"I was minding my own business."

Alana tried to hold back a smile and loudly cleared her throat. They both looked at her.

"Mom, did you see what he did?"

She folded her arms across her chest and nodded. With raised brows, she met Sean's gaze. Only this time, the way he looked at her was different. The raw intensity stole her breath.

She uncrossed her arms and touched her hair. It had to be a mess after a full day's work. Heck, it was always a mess. She cleared her throat again, this time for real. "It smells like you two have been busy," she said breezily as she walked toward the oven. Turning on the light, she peered inside at the golden brown chicken. "Mmm. Looks good."

When she straightened, she found Sean staring at her legs. And not with idle curiosity. She took a deep breath. Had he remembered something? The kiss they'd shared? The mere thought of it made her all warm and tingly. Oh, God. Dare she ask if he had regained some memory?

She forced a smile. "What can I do?"

Sean indicated a kitchen chair with a jut of his chin. "Sit down and put your feet up."

"Don't be silly." She tucked a lock of hair behind her ear. "I can help."

He watched her, his gaze lowering to her throat and then her breasts. When his eyes came back up to lock with hers, the desire there was so raw it made her shockingly wet. "Why don't you relax? You've worked hard all day."

Her pulse sped out of control. "Corey, you go wash up and I'll finish the salad."

"But Mom—"

"Come on, sport, do like your mom says."

With way too much interest, Corey looked from Sean to Alana. He stepped off the stool. "Okay," he said. "Call me when it's time to set the table."

If Alana weren't so hot and bothered, she would have laughed. Her son didn't generally volunteer to do chores. So what the heck was going on? She'd find out, even if it meant she wouldn't have Corey as protection.

She watched him disappear down the hall and waited until she was certain that he was out of earshot. When she faced Sean, she almost lost her nerve.

He was staring at her with a smile that made her knees weak. He put down the potato masher, washed and dried his hands, and then pulled out a kitchen chair. "Come here."

She stayed where she was and flexed her shoulders. "How was your day?" she asked, sounding as no nonsense as possible. "I mean, have you made any progress?"

"Come over here and let me tell you about it." He leaned heavily on the back of the chair, angling toward her.

"I'd really prefer to stand."

His smile turned smug.

She walked to the sink and picked up the vegetable scrubber. "I have a meeting tonight and I'd like to have Corey fed and ready for bed before I leave."

"No problem."

Yes, there was a big problem, she realized as she started on the cucumbers. He was standing behind her, making her feel self-conscious as hell. She tried to concentrate on washing the vegetables and hoped he'd go back to the potatoes. When it appeared he hadn't moved, she finally couldn't stand it another moment and turned around.

He'd left the chair and moved slowly toward her, his intention all too blatant in his eyes.

"Sean? I think we need to talk." She backed up and was thwarted by the sink. "You've remembered something, haven't you?"

He stopped right in front of her and put his hands on her shoulders. She started to protest, but he began kneading her tired muscles and she couldn't recall what she found so objectionable.

"You're tense. Try to relax." He massaged deeper, moved closer.

She let her head drop forward while he ministered to the weary muscles around her nape. His hands were strong and capable as if he'd given a few massages in his time. He kneaded her shoulders, then worked his way around to the front.

"What are you doing?" she asked as he lifted her chin and their eyes met.

"Trying to remember," he said, and pressed his lips to hers.

CHAPTER NINE

SHE TASTED SO INCREDIBLY sweet. Her hair was soft and her skin smelled like vanilla. The way her breasts crushed against his chest made him dizzy with wanting to lie naked beside her in bed. How could he not remember that this beautiful woman was his wife?

He'd felt the connection from day one, but she could have been a girlfriend, or even simply a close friend. But she was his wife...

His hands slid down the curve of her back and over her round firm derriere. She didn't resist, but pressed herself against him. Corey had to have been telling the truth. But why didn't Alana want Sean to know? Probably doctor's orders. Man, they had some weird notions about what a person should be told regarding their own medical condition. That's why he hated hospitals and doctors.

He stiffened. The knowledge was real. Not something fed to him, or something he thought he should know or believe. Sean Everett hated hospitals and doctors. He had little faith in them, and with good reason, but he couldn't quite grasp why...

Alana started to retreat and he pulled her closer. Of course she was reacting to his withdrawal. "Sorry," he murmured as he nipped at her ear. "Just having one of those pesky memory flashes."

She jerked back. "That's wonderful." Her expression went from hopeful to wary. "Do you know who you are? Do you know you're Sean Everett? Are you having actual recall?"

He wouldn't lie, so he shook his head. "That part isn't clear. But I know I hate doctors and hospitals."

She winced. "I'm a vet."

"Not the same."

"Explain." She tried to retreat further, but he locked his arms around her.

"I can't. There's this specific reason why I dread hospitals, but I can't quite wrap my brain around it."

"I suppose that's a start." She glanced over her shoulder.

He took the opportunity to bite her neck.

"Hey, knock it off."

"Corey isn't anywhere in sight. In fact, I can hear him in the bathroom."

"You can't hear from—"

He kissed her. She wiggled a little but it didn't deter him. The little shimmy felt good. *She* felt good. Maybe he ought to lie and tell her he remembered they were married. That they'd been married for less than a year, that he was Corey's stepfather and they were a happy family.

Until the accident.

Damn. Why couldn't he remember?

He moved back, and she slowly opened her eyes, her lips still slightly puckered.

''That feels right,'' he whispered. ''Maybe I am starting to remember.''

She looked a little dazed and then blinked and straightened. ''We're friends, Sean. That's all.''

He didn't answer, only stared at her, studying her face, looking for clues that would unlock his memory.

Her cheeks turned pink. ''I talked to your doctor today,'' she said, slipping between him and the counter and then crossing the kitchen. ''He thinks you need to have some of your own things around you, anything that might trigger your memory. Do you have a friend who could go to your apartment and pick up some—'' She stopped and shook her head. ''Of course you don't remember.''

He watched her get a salad bowl out of the cupboard, his mind swirling in confusion. Why would he have an apartment? Didn't he live here with them? He'd been sleeping in the guest room, but after Corey had dropped the bomb, Sean figured all his stuff must be in Alana's bedroom—*their* bedroom.

''The thing is, I hate going through your personal effects. I wouldn't feel right.'' She got down plates and glasses. ''You have a neighbor who's watering your plants. Maybe I could ask her to—'' She sighed. ''But you probably wouldn't want her digging through your things, either. This is so complicated.''

He almost laughed at the understatement. If he had an apartment and didn't live here, that meant Corey had lied. Or had Sean been a shit and they were separated?

Oh, man, he didn't want to think about that possibility. But why would Corey lie about them being married? Or maybe they'd been married so recently that he hadn't totally gotten out of his apartment yet. No, Corey had said they'd been married almost a year.

"Sean?"

He looked at Alana.

"Do you have an opinion on that?" she asked, her features pinched in a worried frown.

"What?"

She studied him for a moment. "Were you remembering?"

Frustration gripped him, and he shook his head.

"You were so lost in thought, I figured—" She reached for a handful of paper napkins. "It doesn't matter. Don't push yourself. The doctor said the memories should unfold naturally. But we do need to get some of your personal things. And it looks as if I'm it."

Suddenly she looked at him. "Of course, you could go with me and sort through you own things."

He shook his head. "I don't want to leave the house yet."

"Why not?" She studied him closely. "Are you having dizzy spells again?"

"Sometimes I get a little light-headed, but it's not only that." He shrugged. "I just don't feel comfortable going out yet."

"You'll have to go out sometime, to your doctor's appointment, for instance. And it would probably help if you actually saw your apartment."

He exhaled sharply. "I know I'm asking a lot, but would you just bring a few things here?"

She fidgeted with the napkins for a moment, looking indecisive, as if she questioned whether she was doing the right thing. At last she said, "All right."

Sean wasn't sure why he had such a strong aversion to seeing his apartment. Maybe he was afraid he'd remember why Alana had kicked him out. He'd recall the despicable thing he'd done to make her demand a separation.

Or maybe he'd find out that Corey was playing a prank and he really wasn't married to Alana. He hated that thought almost as much. No matter what, she obviously had some affection for him. Her gentleness and patience with him fueled the hope that they had some kind of life together. Or if not, that the possibility existed.

He waited for her to place the napkins on the table and then he took her hand. Surprise leaped into her eyes, and she tensed.

"Why are you doing this?" he asked.

"Doing what?"

"Letting me stay here, following up with my doctors, the whole thing."

"Why wouldn't I? You're a friend."

"I have a feeling there may be a little more than that between us." He noted the anxious way she nibbled at her lower lip, and how she briefly looked away.

"There isn't." She shook her head. "I would tell you if there was a relationship between us, because it could help you remember."

She looked so sincere, yet something was wrong. She seemed uneasy, skittish. Was she afraid of him? No, she wouldn't have him in her house if she were, not with her son here.

Sean sighed heavily. He was going to make himself nuts. He had to let go, let the recall unfold naturally, just as the doctor advised.

"I know it's frustrating, Sean. I can't imagine how horrible it would be to not remember and be at a stranger's mercy. I—I wish I could help."

"Really?"

She looked offended. "Of course."

"Then kiss me."

A startled sound came from somewhere deep in her throat. "What?"

"I'm not being funny or pushy or anything like that. I honestly think it'll help me remember."

"Trust me. It won't." She went back to getting silverware and serving spoons.

"That's the thing…I do trust you. You know, really deep down, beyond memory. Instinctively. I trust you more than if we'd been casual friends."

She looked uncomfortable again. "That's not surprising. Your world is very narrow right now. Basically, all you have are Corey and me."

"True, but I'm talking about fundamental instinct. I trust *you*. The doctors and nurses, for instance, are all people I know I can trust, or should be able to trust. But with you it's different. I know it here." He put his hand against his heart. "I know it down deep."

She stared at his hand for a long moment, and then

hesitantly raised her gaze. "You're under a lot of stress right now. And whether you realize it or not, you are vulnerable."

He took her hand and pulled her close. "Kiss me, Alana."

"Did you listen to anything I just said?"

"Every word." She smelled so sweet, and her eyes were so warm and sincere he wanted to climb inside her, drown in her goodness. "Armchair analysis isn't going to change how I feel about you," he said, and captured her lips before she could protest.

She resisted at first, but then she slid her arms around his neck and pressed her breasts against him. Her heart pounded against his chest. She felt so damn good in his arms, soft and willing. He couldn't get enough of her.

"Sean," she said, pulling away, her face flushed. "This is wrong."

He wouldn't let her go. "Why?"

"I feel like I'm taking advantage of you."

He laughed. "I give you full permission."

"This isn't funny." She looked genuinely troubled. "I won't lie and deny I like kissing you, or having your arms around me or—" She flushed again. "But it isn't right."

"It feels right to me."

"Please, Sean." She touched his cheek, her fingers gentle and lingering. "Don't coax me into doing something I'll regret."

He stared into her eyes for a moment, wanting nothing more than to do just that, but he couldn't. Not with the fear and uncertainty he saw there. He hand no choice but to let her go. For now he'd cling to the hope that blossomed from her loving touch.

SEAN'S APARTMENT TURNED out to be a sunny two-bedroom in a neigborhood similar to Alana's. After unsuccessfully trying to talk his neighbor into gathering some of Sean's things, Alana finally decided to do it herself. She hated the idea of having to go through his possessions, especially after she'd found out about Brenda.

It didn't matter, Alana told herself as she ducked her head into one of the bedrooms. So what that he'd had nearly a two-year relationship with this woman. According to his neighbor, the romance ended five months ago. Sean had been the one to break it off, or so the woman thought, since Brenda had later stopped by several times to see him.

The bedroom had been made into an office, complete with a desk, computer, and filing cabinet. The room was disgustingly neat. Even the paper on his desk was arranged in orderly stacks. The walls were white and bare except for a framed certificate.

She got up close to read the fancy black lettering. It was some kind of award for excellence given to him by the city council. It appeared that he'd handled the renovation of their offices on time and under budget.

Carefully, Alana took the frame off the wall. He had to be proud of the award. Heck, she was surprised that someone as young as Sean had snagged the government contract in the first place. And then to do a job so well that he was publicly commended...

Okay, so he was serious about his work. That didn't change the fact that he was too young for Alana. She looked around the office. His files were meticulously marked and alphabetized, the mail on his desk opened and sorted, but nothing that might be a memory trigger.

She laid the certificate just outside the door to pick up later, and continued on to what she assumed was his bedroom. She smiled at the unmade bed. If it had been all neat and tidy, she'd start wondering about him. She only made hers half the time herself.

Furniture was sparse, consisting of a dresser and one nightstand holding a stack of books that defied gravity. The top one, the latest Stephen King novel, had a bookmark midway through, so she decided to take it with her. She poked through the rest of the books and found a wide assortment of both fiction and nonfiction, many of which she'd read or wanted to read.

There were two framed photos on the dresser, both of Sean and a group of kids horsing around. In one of the pictures, three little boys had him down on the ground, all laughing. She smiled. They were probably his nephews.

She picked up one of them to take with her. She found nothing distinguishable in the attached bathroom, just the usual toiletries. The inside of his closet was one long row of jeans. At the back were two pairs of khakis and a navy blue suit, a couple of dress shirts and several flannel shirts, but that was it.

Her wristwatch beeped, letting her know she had only half an hour before she had to get back to the clinic for her next appointment. She hurriedly gathered what she'd found so far and then went to the living room, where she'd seen more pictures. There were photos of kids of varying ages, and others of Sean.

One photo appeared to have been taken in some exotic tropical locale, with ferns and a waterfall in the distant background. Another looked as if it had been shot at the North Pole. When she examined it more closely, she noticed a sign behind Sean that said Iceland.

Quickly she scanned the rest of the photos. Nearly all were taken in a different foreign location. She shook her head. No wonder he worked so hard. He needed his money for traveling.

Or maybe these were all places he'd lived, and Seattle was just a pit stop for him. But he had started a business here. It shouldn't matter to her and it didn't. She gathered several more pictures, then looked around for anything else that might help. About to leave, she noticed the blinking light on his answering machine.

Automatically she started to press the play button, then hesitated when she realized that it might not be appropriate for her to listen. Then again, there might be an urgent message about work. Alana vacillated for a moment, knowing full well she wanted to hear what was on that answering machine.

No contest. She pressed the button and was subjected to three computer-generated calls, two soliciting

Sean's interest in a security system, and the third, a debt-consolidation loan offer.

The last call was personal. From Brenda, asking to meet for a drink. She wanted him to give them another chance.

Quickly Alana cut off the message, her mood plummeting. Not because she was jealous—but because she'd heard the desperation in the other woman's voice. Sean had dumped her and she was begging him to take her back.

The whole idea made Alana sick to her stomach. Had she sounded like that when Brad had told her he was packing his things and leaving with Sheila?

Alana swallowed around the lump in her throat. She knew better than to relive any of that nonsense. So she'd been hurt. That was over a year ago. Ancient history. And if Sean was cut from the same cloth, it was of no consequence to her, she reminded herself as she shoved the items she was taking into the bag she'd brought.

Even if she were in the market for a serious relationship, Sean was too young. She needed someone more mature, someone who shared her sense of responsibility. How many times did she have to remind herself that Sean wasn't that person? Maybe someday, when he got older…

In the meantime, she hoped they could be friends.

She sighed.

Yeah, right.

"Wow! You brought all this stuff?" Corey stopped unpacking the bag to stare at a picture of Sean and a little girl. "Who's that?"

Alana threw the dish towel on the counter and turned to glare at her son. "Leave Sean's things alone. Would you like it if someone went through your personal belongings?"

He shrugged and poked his nose in the second bag. "I wouldn't care."

"Corey." Her stern tone had him straightening.

"You're back." Sean walked into the kitchen, stretching his arms above his head. His T-shirt rode up to show off a tanned ridge of muscle. "I guess I dozed off."

His gaze went to the two large grocery sacks sitting on the kitchen table, then drifted down to the one on the chair that Corey had his nose in.

"Those are some of your things," she said. "I only brought what I thought might help jog your memory."

"Oh-oh." Corey took one look at Sean and turned pale.

Alana frowned at him. "What's wrong?"

"Nothing." His gaze darted from Alana to Sean. "Can I go out in the backyard?"

"It's almost time for dinner."

"I won't be long."

"What are you going to do?" She glanced over at Sean, who virtually ignored them as he flipped through the pictures.

"Play with the dogs or something."

As she narrowed her gaze on her son, he looked away and started backing up toward the door. One minute ago he couldn't wait to get his hands on Sean's things. Now he looked as if he wanted to catch the next bus to Canada. What the heck was going on?

"Wow!"

Her gaze flew to Sean. He stared at one of the photos, grinning. "You remember something?"

"See you later," Corey said, and ran out the door.

"Don't be long," she called after him, but he'd disappeared so quickly she doubted he heard. She turned back to Sean and waited.

Finally, he set the picture down.

She sighed when he didn't respond. "Well?"

"What?"

"That picture. You reacted. Do you remember anything?"

He shook his head, looking a little sheepish. "No, but it's a cool looking beach."

She rolled her eyes.

"Hey, I can't help it if I don't remember."

True. She turned back to washing the romaine lettuce for their salad. Awful, she knew, but there was a part of her that didn't want Sean to remember too soon. She liked having him around.

He was good company for Corey. And her. Yet the way things stood, there were no strings attached. No promises. No chance for heartache. She was simply helping out a friend.

"Aren't there any pictures of us?"

She looked over her shoulder at him. He was flipping through the rest of the pictures. "Of course not. Why would there be?"

His gaze came up, and she was surprised to see something that looked like resentment flicker in his eyes. "You wouldn't have shown me those, anyway."

"Sean, we haven't known each other that long. There are no pictures of us."

He studied her for a moment, as if trying to decide whether he believed her or not. And then a slow smile lifted his lips. "You'd tell me if we were married, wouldn't you?"

That startled a laugh out of her. "Married? What on earth put that idea into your head?"

He shrugged. "I feel comfortable here. I don't consciously remember anything, yet I go to all the right cupboards and drawers for plates and utensils. I knew exactly where to get trash can liners and filters for the coffeemaker."

She smiled. "And from that you concluded that we're married?"

"Not just that." He moved closer. "I feel comfortable with you."

"We've been through this already." She dodged him and went to the refrigerator for the tomatoes. "Do you remember if you like Italian dressing?" she asked, trying to lighten the situation.

"Thousand Island." His voice was close. His breath stirred her hair. "You smell good," he whispered.

She briefly closed her eyes. She wouldn't turn around. That would be disaster. "Really? I mean, you like Thousand Island?"

"Don't you know?"

It took her a moment to comprehend. "Sean, I

swear to you, we really aren't—'' She turned to face him. Bad move. His lips were a kiss away. ''—married.''

His gaze went straight to her mouth, stayed there for a moment, then lowered to her breasts. He had to notice how hard she was breathing. Apparently he noticed a lot more than that.

His nostrils flared slightly, and he put a hand on her hip. ''Are you sure?''

Her mouth got so dry she could only nod.

''Then let's pretend.'' He kissed her hard, bracketing both her hips, then slid his hands up her sides and drew her into his arms.

God, she felt so right cradled to his chest, Sean thought.

He wanted to believe Corey. Ignore Alana's claims, whether they were accurate or not. He wanted to be her husband. It felt so damn right, how could it be wrong?

''Ouch! My toe—son of a B.'' Corey's voice came from outside the back door.

Sean blinked. And just like that he remembered. Everything.

CHAPTER TEN

ALEXANDRA HAD JUST SLID a small flashlight into her pocket when the doorbell rang. She thought briefly about not answering, but if it were Hannah or Katherine, they'd just start calling her cell phone and panic when she didn't pick up. Where she was going, she was better off traveling light. No phone, no wallet. She did stuff a few five-dollar bills in her pocket for bribes if necessary, then headed for the door.

Hannah waited with an impatient frown that quickly turned to surprise as she looked her friend up and down. "Where the heck are you going dressed like that?"

"Out." Alexandra gave her a pleasant but obstinate smile. "What are you doing here?"

Hannah's brow rose. "Obviously you forgot about dinner."

"What dinner?"

"With Glenda Horn to discuss the center."

"Damn it." Alexandra exhaled sharply. How could she have forgotten something so important? The woman was a potential buyer, for goodness' sakes. She glanced at her watch and then at Hannah.

"May I come in?"

"Do I have a choice?"

Her friend studied her solemnly for a moment, then walked past her into the living room. "I know where you're going."

With a sigh, Alexandra closed the door. "Good for you."

Hannah didn't bat an eye at the sarcasm. "You're going to look for Gary Devlin."

Alexandra looked down at her ragged jeans and faded black T-shirt, the stained and holey tennis shoes that should have been thrown out a year ago. "Gee, what gave me away?"

"This isn't a joke, Alexandra."

"Your point would be?"

Hannah's lips lifted in a sad smile. "The tunnels aren't safe."

"Those people are homeless, not criminals."

"Granted, but some are desperate enough to step off the moral high ground." Hannah spread her hands in a helpless gesture. "Look, we all care about Gary Devlin, but there's only so much we can do for him."

Alexandra turned away to stare out the window. It was getting dark. She'd hoped to reach the tunnels by now. She honestly didn't expect Hannah to understand. Hell, Alexandra herself didn't get what bizarre, inexplicable connection drew her to Gary Devlin, and haunted her dreams. She sent her friend a pleading look. "Hannah, cover for me tonight. Meet with Glenda and then fill me in."

"I have a better idea. Why don't you come with me

to dinner, and then tomorrow night Jack and I will go with you—"

Alexandra shook her head. "I need to go *now*. I haven't seen Gary in a while. He might be hurt."

"Alexandra, please…"

"I'm sorry, Hannah, really I am. I wish I could have gone and come back without you knowing." She grabbed her apartment keys and tried not to buckle under Hannah's frightened look.

"Thanks."

At her sarcasm, Alexandra shot her a wry smile. "I meant so you wouldn't worry."

"Oh, so if you disappeared, we'd never know what happened to you."

"Look." She picked up a sheet of paper she'd left on the counter. "I wrote a note about where I was going."

Hannah's eyes widened.

"You know," Alexandra quickly assured her. "Just in case."

"I'm feeling better and better."

"I'm just trying to show you that I'm not being totally stupid or unreasonable." She saw the skepticism on Hannah's face and held up a small can of pepper spray. "I'm taking this, too."

"Oh, God."

"That is supposed to make you feel better, darn it." Alexandra headed for the door. She needed to leave. Now. Before Hannah talked her out of going. Not that that was likely to happen. When it came to Gary Devlin, Alexandra didn't know the meaning of rational.

"I'VE GOT A CONFESSION to make." Sean waited for Alana to look up from inventorying the drugs she'd just received from UPS.

It took all of two seconds for her to level those pretty green eyes on him. "Yes?"

He tried like the devil not to smile. He should probably feel bad for not admitting he'd regained his memory. But he wasn't ready to be booted out yet. "I know about us."

Her eyebrows drew together. "About us?"

He nodded.

Impatience flickered across her face when he remained silent. "Care to enlighten me?"

He pushed aside the cardboard box she'd just unpacked and hauled himself up to sit on the counter, next to where she worked. "The thing is, I can't tell you how I found out."

"You haven't even told me what you think you know about us."

"Right." He rubbed his jaw, pretending to think about it. "You have to promise you won't slam Corey for this."

"Corey?" She put down her pen. "What did he do?"

"Now, see, you're getting all worked up already."

"I am not."

He grinned. "Then how come you have that little twitch?"

Her eyes widened. "What twitch?"

"The one you get when you're annoyed or upset."

"I do not have a twitch."

"Yeah, you do." He touched the corner of her mouth. "Right there." He let his fingers linger until she moved her head away.

"I don't think that's called a twitch."

"Whatever."

"Quit changing the subject."

"But that's exactly the subject, darlin'. You're going to get upset and blast Corey."

"I'm not getting upset and I won't blast Corey."

"Promise?"

She glared at him. "Yes."

"Cross your heart?"

Her eyes sparked with temper. "Sean."

He smiled. "Come here."

She moved back.

"Come on, Alana, don't be like this. Come here." He paused, took a deep breath so he wouldn't laugh. "After all, we are married."

She stared at him as if he'd grown another head. The array of emotions parading across her face was priceless. She obviously wanted to deny the claim, yet she hesitated, probably fearing to do so would upset him.

He felt a moment's guilt.

"I thought we cleared that up," she said.

"No, you denied it."

"For good reason." She frowned thoughtfully. "Did this memory—how did you arrive at this conclusion, anyway?"

He smiled. He couldn't help it. She was trying to be so rational and professional, but her panicked expression gave her away. "Now, this is the part you promised not to react to, okay?"

Slowly she nodded.

He glanced over his shoulder to make sure Corey hadn't entered the clinic. "Corey told me."

"What?"

"Shh…" He took her arm and drew her closer. "Keep your voice down."

Her skin was so soft, her eyes wide and confused. "What on earth did he tell you?"

"Now, I figure the doctor didn't want you to tell me for some psycho-babble reason, but I'm glad Corey told me. I think it's helping."

"How?" Hope and skepticism fought for control in her eyes. She moved a little closer so that his knee touched her hip, and Sean slid an arm around her waist.

"I felt a connection to you right away. I knew we were more than friends, yet you kept insisting otherwise, and it was confusing."

She stared back at him, clearly uncertain what to say next. He probably should tell her the truth…

Lifting a hand, she gently touched the scraped and bruised area at his hairline. "How are the headaches?"

"Mostly gone."

"And your elbow?"

He'd banged it up pretty good trying to break the fall. "It's still achy and stiff, but better."

Her fingers moved into his hair, and he closed his eyes, basking in her warmth, relishing the feeling of complete and utter contentment. "I have to tell you something," she said, "something not very pleasant."

He opened his eyes, but didn't say anything.

She lowered her hand. "I don't know why Corey told you we were married. He's been— It doesn't matter. The truth is, we aren't married, Sean. We really are just friends."

"But—" He tried to look confused while he gathered his thoughts. God, he was a jerk for not telling her he knew, that he remembered everything. But in another week he'd be healed enough to return to work. He'd leave then. Go back to his lonely apartment.

She shook her head. "I can't tell you why he did it. Maybe he thought it would help you get better, or maybe…I just don't know."

"He probably thinks you need the company. Obviously, since he—" Sean cut himself short. He'd almost blown it by mentioning the auction.

Her eyes were warm and innocent as she looked expectantly at him.

He had to tell her the truth. She had a right to know that he remembered, a right to kick him out and reclaim her privacy. He moved closer to the edge of the counter and spread his legs further apart. Sliding an arm around her waist, he maneuvered her to a spot in front of him. She didn't resist, so he drew her closer, slipping his other arm around her and nestling her between his thighs.

She put her hands on his shoulders and sighed. "Sean, do you understand what I've told you?"

He nodded, slanted his mouth over hers and kissed

her gently. Her hands tightened on his shoulders, and he increased the pressure on her lips. He would tell her...in just a minute...

She slid her arms around his neck and pressed her breasts against his chest. A groan escaped him. His hand molded the curve of her buttocks.

"Sean, we shouldn't," she said, pulling back slightly.

"Why not?" He lightly bit her earlobe.

"Because."

He chuckled. "Pick that snappy response up from Corey, did you?"

She smiled and tilted her head back to give him better access to her neck. "Speaking of whom...he should be getting home soon."

Sean licked the line of her jaw. "Then I guess we'd better hurry."

She laughed softly. "It means we'd better stop."

Her words said one thing, Sean thought, but her body said quite another. Molded to him the way she was, she'd have no doubt about his physical interest. Not even that cooled her off. If anything, she seemed more eager, her mouth seeking his.

"Alana?"

Her lashes fluttered and then her eyes slowly opened. God, he was going to regret this. "I think Corey may be home," he said, reluctantly drawing back. "I thought I heard a door slam."

She blinked. "Corey?" Her gaze flew to her watch. "Oh, my God, I didn't realize it was that late."

She pushed away from Sean, nearly sending him

backward against the wall. He caught her by the wrist before she could get too far.

"Hold on. It's not like we're doing anything wrong."

The look she gave him was long and searching. "I'm sorry that Corey misled you. I truly am. But I will not do anything that will jeopardize his welfare."

"Whoa." Sean slid off the counter. "We seem to have had a communication breakdown. You think I don't want what's best for Corey?"

Her shoulders sagged. "Of course not. I only meant that he's my first priority, and I can't have him walking in on us like this."

He tried not to smile. "Like what?"

"I'm serious, Sean. I don't want him getting his hopes up."

"Hell, my hopes were up."

"Everything is a big joke to you."

"Not everything."

She sighed. "Right."

Sean was an inch from telling her he'd recovered his memory. That he remembered how much he'd admired her dedication to Corey, that he admired her as an independent woman. But selfish bastard that he was, he kept his mouth shut. It would kill him to be booted out of her life now. This was his chance to show her he was serious…serious about exploring a relationship between them.

"You think this is just about sex, don't you?"

That got her attention. She stared at him, eyes wide

and indignant. "No." Her chin came up. "Maybe. I don't know, Sean. But it doesn't matter."

"Of course it matters." That ticked him off. "It sure as hell matters to me."

Her expression softened. "I only meant that—"

"I know what you meant, Alana. You're afraid of having a relationship and you use Corey as a shield."

"That is not true!"

Their gazes dueled. He refused to speak, wanting her to think about what he'd said.

"You don't understand because you aren't a parent," she said quietly, her eyes sparking fire.

"So you've told me." He shook his head. "You give me so little credit."

"This isn't about you."

"You're right." Any man interested in her would face the same obstacles she threw up with impunity. "But I'll tell you something I know for certain. If you thought for one moment I was a bad influence or posed any kind of threat to Corey, I wouldn't have made it through the front door."

She looked away. "True."

"So cut me some slack, would you?"

Her sigh was one of disgust. "Believe me, you've had a lot of slack. A lot more than—" She cut herself off and turned back to recording her drug shipment. "I really do have to get back to work."

He smiled, his ego nicely stroked, knowing that she'd been about to admit he'd gotten more than his foot in the door. "One more thing." She cast him an impatient look, but he continued, "If Corey wanted me to believe that we're married, don't you think that's something you should be concerned about?''

Now she glared at him. "Of course I'm concerned. He knows better than to lie."

He shook his head. "I'm talking about concern for why he felt the need to lie."

"What are you getting at?"

Sean shrugged casually. "Maybe we should go along, keep up the pretense. Find out what the problem is."

Her gaze narrowed. "Pretend we are married?"

He nodded. Alana dropped her pen. "Are you crazy?"

"Right now that would be a good assessment. But concerning this problem with Corey, I think I have a point, and if you'd quit being so defensive, you might understand."

She stared blankly at him. "You are kidding, right?"

He shook his head, his gaze fastened to hers.

"Sean, I know you mean well…" She made a soft sound of helplessness. "I appreciate your concern, really."

"But you think I'm full of crap."

"I wouldn't put it that way."

"Okay, so you don't think I know what I'm talking about because I don't have kids."

She pressed her lips together. "It's not easy being a parent."

"Hell, I know that." He almost reminded her that they'd had this discussion that first night at dinner, but caught himself. "Some day I hope to experience that problem firsthand."

"I have no doubt that some day you will."

"Just not with you."

Her eyes became guarded. "For what it's worth, if you were older and settled, if the situation were different, I think you'd make a fine father and husband."

His defenses shot up. What was this age hang-up? And then he saw it…the flicker of longing in her eyes. And hope rose again.

ALEXANDRA STUMBLED IN THE darkness and patted her pockets for the small flashlight she'd brought. She'd hoped she wouldn't have to use it, but despite her earlier bravado when talking with Hannah, the tunnels scared the bejeezus out of her.

It was dark and gloomy down here, and the damp moldy smell made her heart race and her hands tremble. She withdrew the pencil-thin flashlight, but before she could flick it on, it slipped from her clammy fingers. Staying perfectly still, she tried to judge where it fell as it clanked against the rocks.

Slowly she crouched down and patted the ground with her palms. Slimy, disgusting textures had her bolting upright. She'd make do without the flashlight.

As she made her way deeper into the tunnels, the putrid odor of smoke and unwashed bodies assailed her and she pulled the neckline of her shirt up to cover her mouth and nose.

Occasionally she'd see a small campfire, and it took every ounce of courage not to run back the way she'd come. Although she didn't remember that much about the night her home burned to the ground, for the past twenty years the sight and smell of fire had haunted her, making her sick to her stomach.

The warning that the tunnel residents had been given against the use of fire seemed to mean little. Most of them had suffered the devastation of the last tunnel fire, but they needed to keep warm and occasionally have a hot meal, so survival overruled caution.

She sighed, took another quick breath and pulled up her neckline again. At least the campfires showed her the way. God only knew if she'd have made it this far without breaking a leg.

"What do you want here?"

The gruff voice startled her and she slid down a slick slope, twisting her ankle. She settled on an uncomfortable rock and peered into the darkness. "I can't see you."

"You have no business here, girlie."

"I'm looking for someone." She thought she saw an outline of a person but couldn't be sure. "I don't mean any harm."

"Ain't nobody down here that should interest a girl like you."

Girl like her? At this curve in the tunnel, it was blacker than a moonless midnight sky. This person couldn't possibly see her. Had he been following her?

"He's a friend and I'm worried about him," Alexandra said, probing her ankle and squinting into the darkness. "I just want to make sure he's all right."

After a lengthy silence, she heard a mild oath, and then, "Who might this fellow be?"

The gruff voice belonged to a woman, Alexandra realized. The discovery made her feel marginally better, although why she didn't know. A woman could be equally dangerous, especially in this black hellhole.

"Gary Devlin. Do you know him?" She held her breath as the woman paused.

"I might." The woman stepped forward and shone a small light in Alexandra's eyes.

She drew back, her hand coming up to block the intrusive glare.

"Let me see your face," the woman demanded, keeping the light in Alexandra's eyes.

Alexandra squinted and lowered her hand.

"How do you know Gary?"

"Like I said, I'm a friend of his."

The woman made a disgusting hacking sound. "Why haven't I seen you before?"

"Would you please lower that light a little?" Alexandra asked. "Just so I'm not blinded."

"You better not try anything funny, girlie."

"No, I just want to make sure Mr. Devlin is all right."

It was as if Alexandra had discovered the magic password. Immediately the light was lowered. The woman's outline was still shadowy in the darkness, but at least she stayed put and kept the flashlight aimed at the slimy ground.

"How do you know Gary?" she asked again.

"My friends and I own a day care-center and—"

"Are you Alexandra?"

The light shot up, blinding her again, and she put up her hand. "Yes."

"Why didn't you say so? You're pretty just like he said." The woman grunted and flashed the beam away. "I'm Stella. Follow me."

There was no time for a response. Stella was bulky but she could move. It took some doing for Alexandra to keep up with her and not slip on the slimy ground.

Fortunately, Stella stopped about a hundred yards further down the tunnel. She shone the light on a wooden crate and well-worn sleeping bag. Another heap of clothes and books were stashed beside a large rock. "That's Gary's stuff."

"Where is he?" Alexandra wrapped her arms around herself as she squinted into the darkness, trying to see.

Stella shrugged. "Probably gone to look for something to eat."

"Guess I'll just wait here." She shivered at the thought, but she wouldn't be happy until she actually saw him and knew he was all right.

"I can tell him you came by. Go on home. This ain't no place for you to hang around, girlie."

"This isn't a place for anyone, Stella." Alexandra sighed, hoping the woman hadn't taken offense. "I have to see him for myself. Make sure he's okay. Not that I don't trust what you said," she added quickly.

Stella stood quietly for a moment, then held out the light. "Here."

Not sure what the woman meant, Alexandra stared at it.

"Take it."

"Your flashlight? What about you?"

"I got me another one just yesterday." She reached into her overcoat and flicked on a small key chain light. "You give that one to Gary when you see him. He'll make sure it gets back to me."

"Thanks." Alexandra gratefully accepted the light.

She touched Stella's hand and the woman jerked until she realized Alexandra just wanted to shake it.

"You shouldn't be touching me, girlie. I'm grimy as hell."

"So am I." She squeezed Stella's hand and was able to discern a smile on the woman's dirty face. "I'll make sure you get the light back."

Stella squeezed her hand back and then disappeared into the darkness.

The small flashlight illuminated Gary's things. The subhuman conditions that the tunnel people lived in made Alexandra's heart heavy. It wasn't as if she hadn't been aware of their plight, but standing here and witnessing their misery was a hard pill to swallow.

Needing reassurance that she was waiting for the right person, she skimmed the light over the meagre stack of clothes and personal effects. Gary had held on to a surprising number of books, which made her all the more curious about him. Even more interesting was that two of them were law volumes. The other three were dog-eared paperbacks by pop-fiction authors.

Beside the books was an old shoebox. The lid sat loosely on top and Alexandra wanted like crazy to have a peek inside. She got closer but talked herself out of being so nosy. Gary had a right to his privacy. The poor man possessed little else.

She glanced over her shoulder in the direction from which she'd come, the mouth of the tunnel. He'd probably be coming from that way, too, she figured, but looked for a smooth dry spot on the rocks where she could sit and watch both directions.

It didn't hurt that she had a solid cement wall behind her that eliminated anyone approaching without warning. She slid a hand between her lower back and the wall, testing the structure before leaning back. As she did so, the beam of light flashed jerkily and picked out something odd on the rocks.

Steadying the flashlight, she shone it around the small area. What she noticed was a doll. A really old, faded and battered doll with blond string hair and glassy eyes. What the hell would Gary Devlin be doing with a doll? Maybe this wasn't his stuff.

She scrambled to her feet again, not sure if she should stick around or keep looking for Gary.

But something about the doll nagged at her, and she swung the flashlight back to illuminate it again. The pink mouth had faded, but at the corners were faint traces of red paint where someone had tried to extend the smile.

A painful lump lodged in her throat and she gasped for air. That was her doll—Mary Jane. She'd gotten it for her fifth birthday. One that looked just like it, anyway.

Her heart pounded and sweat broke out above her lip. Obviously it couldn't be the same doll. Hers had been lost in the fire. This probably wasn't even Gary's camp.

But the red smile lines...? Could another child have thought to do the same thing?

She heard someone whistling behind her and turned around to see a circle of light approaching. The whistling stopped abruptly.

"Who's there? Get away from my things." It was Gary's voice, all right.

If this *was* her doll, what the hell was he doing with it?

No, it couldn't be. The doll had perished in the fire. She had so few memories of that night…the flames… the suffocating smoke. But she remembered standing at the railing at the top of the staircase, scared out of her mind as the flames grew higher, the doll clutched in her hands.

"Who's there?" Gary demanded again as he got closer. "Alexandra?"

She opened her mouth to answer, but her voice wouldn't work. The shadows on the rock wall blurred together. A drowning sensation swept over her and her knees buckled.

"Alexandra, what's wrong?"

That's the last thing she heard before she sank into oblivion.

SUNLIGHT STREAMED IN between the blinds, warming Alexandra's face. She yawned and stretched. A sharp pain shot through her head, and she raised her hand to the base of her skull, where the pain had started. Her fingers met with a small lump and she suddenly remembered last night. In the tunnels.

Gary Devlin.

Her doll.

Passing out.

That must have been when she'd hit her head.

She gazed around the room…her room, and then down at the same clothes she'd worn last night. Someone had brought her here.

Gary. It had to be him.

She listened for a moment but heard nothing. She

called out, and still nothing. Whoever had brought her home was probably long gone by now. She stared at the ceiling, her thoughts a tangled mess of impossibilities. She glanced at the clock, then reached for her bedside phone.

It was still early in Texas, but she had to talk to Mitch Barnes. Mitch worked for Finders Keepers, a company that specialized in reuniting families. Hannah had used the agency, which was started by her friend Dylan Garrett, to help her find the son she'd given up for adoption. Alexandra needed to pass on this new information to Mitch. She knew he'd slowed down on the case, become resistant after the FBI had contacted her.

Screw them. They'd warned her to quit digging up information on Gary. That alone had made her curious. But now there was the doll....

Mitch had to help her. He'd once worked for the FBI himself. He had contacts there. He couldn't give up. No matter what.

CHAPTER ELEVEN

"WHAT'S A LEMUR?" Ritchie asked as he peered over the railing on tiptoe, searching for the elusive animals. The Seattle zoo was crowded, even for a Sunday, and several pairs of youthful eyes turned to look at Alana and Sean for the answer.

"Don't you know?" Corey rolled his eyes, and with a superior air added, "Everyone knows they're sort of like a monkey."

Ritchie's face got red. "You always think you know everything."

Alana was about to admonish Corey for being rude, but Sean stepped in.

"I didn't know what a lemur was until a few years ago," he said, shrugging. And then he looked directly at Corey. "Not everyone has a mother who's a veterinarian. Because of that, you get to learn more about animals than most people."

Corey scrunched up his nose and thought about it for a moment. "Yeah, I guess."

"You're pretty lucky, don't you think?"

"Yeah, you're lucky," Ritchie said. "I wish my mom knew about monkeys and tigers and stuff like that."

"That's okay," Sean told him. "I'd bet Corey would like to share what he knows with you."

"Sure." Corey's grin stretched wide. "Come on, Ritchie, I'll tell you about the baboons."

Alana watched the boys scamper off to the next exhibit before she turned to Sean. "Well done."

He blinked, clearly surprised. "What?"

"How you handled Corey. You didn't embarrass him but you made a point."

"Heck, I don't like being embarrassed. I sure wouldn't do it to him."

She smiled. "You're a natural."

He smiled back. "Yeah?"

"Yeah."

"I guess I've learned a few tricks with my nieces and nephews over the years."

Alana noticed that he kept an eye on the boys while he talked with her, and his concern warmed her. This wasn't the first time she'd been touched by his regard for Corey. Last evening when the three of them had gone out for ice cream, they'd stopped at a nearby playground. Sean had barely taken his gaze off Corey, and as soon as it started getting dark, it was Sean who suggested they leave. He acted more like a father to Corey than Brad ever had.

Dangerous thinking. Very dangerous. For both Corey and her.

The past few days had been like balancing on a tightrope. Although they never again discussed Corey's lie or Sean's ridiculous suggestion that they fulfill his wish, they'd carried on very much like a family.

The three of them had grocery shopped, eaten dinner together every night, gone to the movies, and argued over the remote control and which programs to watch. Corey had been like a different child. Happy and smiling all the time. And damn it, but Alana had started wearing a little makeup again.

Dangerous and stupid.

"Hey, you guys, those animals aren't going anywhere." Sean motioned for the boys to slow down.

They immediately obeyed, and waited for Sean and Alana to catch up. She didn't mind that Sean spoke up like he did. He never overstepped his bounds by trying to discipline Corey. She certainly wouldn't have stood for that sort of interference, but she did welcome his concern.

"Are we gonna eat soon?" Corey asked as soon as they approached.

Alana laughed and looked at her watch. "You just had breakfast."

Corey rushed over to peer at Sean's watch. He studied the hands for a moment. "That was three whole hours ago."

Alana gasped. "When did you learn how to tell time?"

"Sean's been teaching me." Corey grinned with pride. "He said it's cheating to look at a digi—digi—"

"Digital." Sean winked at her.

"Digital watch. He said I needed to know how to

read a regular one.'' Corey gave Ritchie a smug look.
"He's going to buy me my own wristwatch.''

"Cool.'' Ritchie eyed Sean's watch with envy. "I
can't tell time yet.''

Sean noisily cleared his throat to get Corey's attention. "But you get it on what condition?''

"Huh?''

"What do you have to do to earn the watch?''

Corey's long-suffering sigh made Alana smile, although she wasn't thrilled with the idea that Sean had
made the offer. It didn't matter if it were only a five-
dollar watch, she wanted him to check with her before
buying Corey things. God, she hoped she knew what
the heck she was doing by letting Sean into their lives.

"I have to be able to tell time,'' Corey said, starting
to fidget, his attention wandering toward the elephants.

"What else?''

"I have to do it in seconds.''

"Close.'' Sean wouldn't let up. "When you can
look at the hands and tell me what time it is before
two seconds are up, you get your own watch.'' Sean
looked at her. "What do you think, Mom? Does that
sound reasonable?''

"I guess so.'' She smiled at Corey. She had a few
words for Sean, but they could wait till later.

"Okay.'' Sean stared at his watch. "Ready?''

Corey positioned himself so he could see the face,
his hand wrapped around Sean's larger, tanned arm.
"Ready.''

"One, two, three— Go!''

Corey froze. His face creased in a frustrated frown. "Twenty after eleven."

"You got the time right, buddy." Sean gave him an encouraging smile. "But it took you five seconds."

Corey's expression fell.

"Hey, you're getting better." Sean put up his hand and Corey delivered an unenthusiastic high five. "This morning it took you six seconds. Come on. Again."

This time Corey grinned and slammed his palm against Sean's.

"I wanna earn a watch, too," Ritchie whined. "Can I?"

"Come on, guys." Alana cut in, although she thought briefly about letting Sean get out of his own mess. "Let's head toward a snack bar if you want some lunch."

"I want a hot dog," Corey said, "and potato chips and my own cola."

"I want a cheeseburger and French fries." Ritchie started walking backward and Alana turned him around in time to avoid colliding with a woman pushing a stroller.

Sean grunted. "I'm having a hot dog and a cheeseburger and French fries and maybe even two colas."

The two boys exchanged wide-eyed glances. "Wow!"

Alana laughed as she herded the boys in the right direction. When she looked over at Sean, she caught him watching her. "What's wrong?"

He shook his head. "I like it when you smile or laugh. Your whole face lights up."

"It's not like I don't do either often."

"Not nearly enough."

At his continued scrutiny, her cheeks began to heat up. "Boys, settle down," she said, hoping to divert Sean's attention.

Corey gave her a funny look. "We're not doing nothing."

"You're not doing anything."

"Yeah, I know."

Sean hooted with laughter, and she gave him a playful punch in the arm. He captured her fist and kissed the back of her hand. Corey caught the interchange and his eyes sparkled with happiness.

She promptly pulled away, but not before she heard Sean whisper, "Later."

COREY RUBBED HIS EYES, and Ritchie yawned widely as they headed for the zoo exit. It was obvious both boys were tired, but selfishly, Sean didn't want the day to end. They'd been like a real family. Other than the times he'd spent with his nieces and nephews, he'd never felt so much like he belonged. More important, he'd never seen Alana more relaxed.

She was sipping the last of her lemonade so she could throw the cup into the trash can they were approaching. Her nose was pink from the sun, even though she'd slathered sun block over herself and the boys.

With a grin, he recalled the look on her face when he'd asked her to rub some on him. She'd been the one who suggested it would be wise to coat the exposed areas of his skin. He'd pulled off his T-shirt, offered her his bare shoulder and told her to rub away. Her eyes wide, she'd handed him the tube and disappeared.

If it weren't for Corey, Sean would swear she was still a virgin. She embarrassed so easily, and man, was she ever skittish. He understood that she worried Corey would see or hear something between them he shouldn't. Sean didn't blame her. He wanted to be cautious, too. Just not overly cautious. Hell, the kid could be visiting Siberia and she'd probably worry he'd find them in a compromising position. Of course, Sean realized her wariness wasn't only about Corey. The problem was far bigger than that.

"Hey, Corey, Ritchie, how tired are you guys?" he asked, and Alana slid him a look that shot daggers.

"Why?" Corey asked around a yawn.

"Are you crazy?" Alana rolled her eyes. "They're tired, period. The sun is already setting and we're probably the last to leave the zoo. We're going straight home."

"But—" Corey and Sean began at the same time.

"No discussion." They'd already crossed the nearly empty parking lot and Alana clicked the remote and unlocked the doors of her Ford Explorer. She opened one in the back. "Come on, boys, get in."

"Good," Sean whispered as he passed by her. "Let's put them to bed so we can be alone."

"Right." Her laugh sounded ragged. He smiled and opened the passenger door, then walked around to the driver's side.

She buckled both boys in and looked questioningly at Sean over the roof of the car. "What are you doing?"

"Tonight I'm chauffeuring you."

"Not a good idea."

"Why not?"

"Your head—you're not healed..."

"I'm fine to drive, Alana, I promise you." He put up a hand when she started to protest again. "Do you think I would endanger you or Corey, or even Ritchie?"

Their gazes locked for several long moments, and then she tossed the keys over the roof.

He nearly missed them but snagged the remote with his left hand. "Thanks."

As he climbed behind the wheel, a strong surge of emotion caught him off guard, making him a little shaky, and for a second he considered having her drive, after all. It seemed a small thing, letting him take the wheel, but for Alana the gesture was anything but casual.

If she had a fault, to Sean's way of thinking, it was that she was often overprotective of Corey. A control issue, obviously, in the same way she tried to control her own emotions where Sean was concerned. The more she learned to trust him, the more she'd let go. This evening was the first step.

Hell, maybe tonight would be *the* night.

Sean tried not to gun the engine in his hurry to get home.

"BUT WHAT ARE YOU GUYS gonna do?" Corey asked as Alana pulled the covers up to his chin. On the other twin bed, Ritchie was already asleep, his purring snore tamer now that she'd given him his allergy pill.

"What difference does it make, young man? You nearly fell asleep over dinner and yawned through your entire bath."

"So."

She shook her head. "I'm going to read, and Sean will probably watch TV."

Yeah, right. But these types of fibs didn't count. She couldn't very well tell her son they were going to do "adult things."

She shivered at the thought.

"Are you cold, Mommy?" Corey asked, his eyes sleepy. "You can get in bed with me for a while."

"Nope." She kissed him on the forehead and then on the chin. "You go to sleep or else Ritchie will wake up all rested and ready to go fishing with Sean and you'll be too tired."

"Never."

"I don't know about that…"

He promptly closed his eyes and squeezed them tight.

Smiling, she kissed him once more and then whispered, "Good night."

He didn't say a word, and she wouldn't be surprised if he were already half-asleep. She peeked at Ritchie, his mouth slightly open, his strawberry-blond hair poking up over the pillow, and then she stopped in the bathroom to check her own mop before meeting Sean in the living room.

There was no hope for her hair. The humid Seattle evening had done a number on it. Unless she wanted to wash it and blow it dry again, she had little option but to tie it back, or continue looking like a wild woman. She bound it in a loose ponytail, and then went to help Sean finish cleaning the kitchen.

He stood at the sink, polishing off the leftover casserole they'd heated for dinner. The rest of the kitchen was clean, the counters clear, the dishes washed and put away. Only one pot remained in the sink, soaking—the one with the burned-on tomato-sauce stains.

"I told you I'd help," she said as he put the last forkful of cheesy pasta into his mouth.

"That casserole was awesome. If we weren't already married, I'd ask you to marry me."

She shook her head and smiled. She'd miss his teasing when he left. Of course, he wasn't going far, but admittedly, she'd gotten comfortable with their nightly routine and joking.

"Looks like you got more sauce on your mouth than in your tummy," she said, handing him a paper towel.

"Want to lick it off?"

She gave him a stern look as she turned to gather the dish towels so he couldn't see her smile.

"Can't blame me for trying." He wiped his mouth. "How do I look?"

Good enough to eat. She didn't dare voice her initial

thought. He needed little encouragement as it was. "Like a grown-up again."

"That's scary."

She sighed. *Men.* "Hand me the dishrag, would you? I'm going to put in a load of laundry."

He took the dish towels out of her hand. "No, you aren't. I'm doing laundry tomorrow afternoon while you're at the clinic. The boys are all tucked in and counting sheep by now, I take it?"

"Yes, but—"

He took her by the shoulders and turned her toward the living room. "Good, because we're going to sit and have a relaxing evening together."

"But I have personal laundry to do."

"Which happens to be my specialty." He guided her into the living room, not releasing her until they reached the couch.

"You don't understand." She turned to face him, his mere nearness making her start to feel warm. "I mean *really* personal laundry, as in *my* personal laundry."

His eyes lit with amusement. "Sweetheart, I've seen panties before."

"Fine, but you aren't washing mine."

He laughed. "How about if I keep my eyes closed while I load the washer?"

She laughed, too. "Okay, I won't do any laundry right now, but you don't touch mine. Got it?"

"Got it."

"Good." She sat down on the couch. "But honestly, you don't have to do the laundry. It's easy for me to throw a load in after I leave the clinic.''

"It's even easier for me. I'll be here all afternoon after the boys and I get back from fishing. I have several calls to make—jobs I have to reschedule, which usually means waiting around for return calls.''

She stared at him. "Rescheduling jobs? How do you know—have you remembered something?''

Frowning, he rotated his shoulder and then stretched, his gaze darting away. "The doc said I should regain my memory soon, right? So I have to start thinking about getting back in the saddle.''

"But you shouldn't push yourself, either.''

He looked amused as he sat beside her, close, their legs touching, and then he slid his arm around the back of the couch. "Why? Are you going to miss me?''

"Corey certainly will.''

"What about you?''

"Of course.'' She met his teasing eyes. "Then I'll have to start cooking again and doing laundry.''

"Honest?''

"What?''

"Is that the only reason you'd miss me?'' The curve of his mouth indicated he already knew the answer.

"Do you have any idea how unattractive conceit is?''

He laughed so loudly she had to shush him. "You wake the boys and they're all yours.''

"Are you kidding? They're so pooped a sonic boom wouldn't wake them.'' He angled his head to look her fully in the eyes. "Which makes me wonder— Why did you pull your hair back?"

"Because it's a mess. Talk about a non sequitur. Going from sonic boom to my hair." She paused for a moment's thought. "Or should I take offense?"

"Nope. I like it a mess." He pulled the elastic band free.

She stiffened against the insane desire to curl into him, to let him hold her, kiss her, and make her forget she was a single mom with a steep mortgage and a jerk of an ex-husband.

"And it's not at all a non sequitur," he continued. "If the boys are that sound asleep—" he twirled a lock of her hair around his finger "—and you're looking this sexy…"

Her stomach somersaulted. "What's on TV?"

She reached for the program guide, but before she could lean back again, he had his arms around her, his lips on her neck, trailing tiny kisses up to her ear. He stopped at the sensitive spot behind her lobe that drove her crazy and nibbled the skin.

"Sean." She angled away but he persisted. "Come on, Sean."

"What's your excuse now, Alana?" he whispered, moving his lips to her nape.

She nearly moaned with pleasure. "I don't need an excuse. I just don't want to."

"What? Make out?"

When she felt his smile against her skin, she couldn't help but laugh. "I haven't heard that term in a while."

"Maybe you need a refresher course. I'd be happy to show you how it's done." He used his tongue to forge a trail to her mouth.

Closing her eyes, she let her head fall back. "This, you remember how to do," she murmured, pretty darn glad he did.

"Kind of like riding a bike." He sucked in her lower lip between his teeth and bit down gently.

Instinctively she opened her mouth, and he slid his tongue inside. She kissed him back, and didn't object when his hand slipped down to cup her breast. He kneaded gently while kissing her thoroughly, and heat spread through her chest, down her belly and between her thighs.

He pulled back slightly, and she whimpered.

"Alana, you taste so good." He kissed the side of her neck. "You smell good. You're incredible. God, I want to make love to you all night."

She nearly lost her ability to breathe altogether. She sucked in air and closed her eyes. Why not go for it? No empty promises. No strings. Just mind-boggling sex. Sean could deliver, of that she had no doubt.

"Alana," he whispered in her ear like a caress. "We'd be so good together."

Slowly she opened her eyes, trying to think, trying to interpret his words. Good together for the night? He couldn't be thinking long term. That would never work.

"Sean, let's talk." Her voice came out so breathless he had to be laughing inside.

"I'd rather do this." He licked the shell of her ear

and then nipped her lobe, using just enough pressure to make her want to grab for him.

"Me, too," she admitted. "But we have to talk—" she swallowed hard "—first."

He stopped and looked at her, his eyes glazed with desire. "All right," he said after a moment, his fingers making abstract designs on her sensitive skin.

The phone rang.

She jerked. It never rang. At least, not at this time of night.

"Let it go." Sean moved to kiss her.

She ducked. "It'll wake the boys."

"No way."

"I have to answer, Sean. It could be an emergency. The clinic line is forwarded here at night." She got up before he tried to discourage her.

But he only nodded and sat back. Refreshing. Brad had always pitched a fit when her patients' owners called her at home. He'd say she wasn't a *real* doctor and that he didn't see the necessity of keeping hours beyond five. It had taken her a year to realize what he'd really meant—that he wanted to hang out in bars or at the basketball court with his friends instead of having to watch his son.

As soon as Alana saw the phone number on the caller ID display, her stomach turned over. She hesitated picking it up, but quickly realized that Brad would probably leave an obnoxious message and Sean would hear it, so she grabbed the receiver.

"Dr. Fletcher," she answered, because she knew it would annoy the hell out of Brad.

Silence.

Her back to Sean, she smiled triumphantly. "Hello? This is Dr. Fletcher."

"It's me."

"Pardon?"

"Damn it, Alana, I know you have caller ID, so cut the crap."

That remark earned a wider smile. "Brad?"

He grunted. "I'm not in a good mood."

"What's new?" She sighed at her own sarcasm. This wasn't worth it. "What can I do for you?"

"Where's Corey?"

"In bed, and I'm not waking him. You know you should call earlier."

"Relax, honey. I wanted to talk to you. I just didn't want him listening."

She started to tell him he'd lost the right to call her honey, but remembered just in time that Sean was within earshot. "What is it?"

"You don't have to be so curt."

"I have company."

"Oh, yeah. Who?"

"No one you know."

"A man?"

"None of your business." She slid a sidelong glance at Sean. He seemed preoccupied leafing through one of her periodicals on modern veterinary medicine, but he had to be listening. "I suggest you tell me why you called."

Brad hesitated. No doubt he wanted to ask her more about her male companion, but he wouldn't, because he knew how stubborn she could be. "It's about next weekend."

She frowned. Next weekend? They hadn't arranged a visit. "What about it?"

"I think I might be in Seattle for a day, but I'm not sure yet."

"You're going to drive up for only one day?"

"Nah, it's business. I'd fly up in the morning and I figured I'd see Corey at the same time."

She should have known Brad wasn't coming just for Corey, but bit down on her lip to keep from making a nasty remark. "He has a birthday party to go to Saturday afternoon, but other than that he's free."

"Yeah, well, I figured I'd just take him to dinner Friday evening before I flew home."

"Brad, you can't be serious."

"You wanted me to see him. I thought you'd be pleased."

"You want to see him for only an hour or so?"

He made a sound of disgust. "There you go, making me out to be the bad guy again. I didn't say that's all I wanted to see him for…that's simply all the time I have."

She closed her eyes against the hot tears welling up. Corey didn't deserve this. He was a good kid. But she wasn't going to change Brad. She wasn't going to make him want to see his son.

She hadn't even been able to make him love her.

"Right." She silently cleared her throat. "Fine. Let me know when you find out your travel plans."

"Don't tell him yet, okay? Just in case our client settles out of court and the trip isn't necessary."

It was all she could do to keep from screaming at him. Visiting his son was necessary. Why didn't he get it? She took a deep breath. "Of course."

"Thanks, honey. I should know tomorrow, and I'll go ahead and tell my secretary to book a later flight home. Then you can tell Corey."

"Okay." She hung up. He'd still been on the line but she didn't care. Better to cut off the conversation than say something she'd regret.

"Alana?"

She heard Sean's voice and realized she'd been staring at the phone for at least a minute. She chased away the depressing thoughts of Brad and turned around.

"You okay?"

"Fine." She managed a small smile. "Can I get you something?"

"No." His gaze stayed on her. "Can I get you something?"

"Tequila. Two shots. No salt."

"Really?"

She sighed. "I'm kidding."

"Probably wouldn't be a bad idea."

She shook her head. "It's time for me to turn in." Coward that she was, she glanced at the mantel clock rather than at the disappointment in Sean's face, then headed for the hall.

"Alana, wait."

She didn't turn around. Not even when she heard him say, "You can't always run away."

CHAPTER TWELVE

SEAN OPENED THE OFFICE door just as Alexandra picked up the phone. She motioned him inside, so he walked in and took a chair near the window. A group of children were playing in the fenced-in front yard.

Corey wasn't there. Sean would have spotted that mop of blond hair immediately. Amazing how many people mistook him for Corey's father. Sean's unruly hair wasn't nearly as blond as Corey's, but just as much a pain, always falling down his forehead and getting in his eyes.

On several occasions when someone at the fish market or hardware store had assumed Corey was his son, Sean had let the mistake pass. Man, he could be really happy with a kid like Corey and a wife like Alana.

He breathed in deeply. Not just a woman *like* Alana. He wanted her. Alana Fletcher. The best mom and veterinarian in the world. And she had damn fine legs. Fine everything. He wanted the entire package. Why else would he abandon his pride and be sitting here, waiting to ask for another woman's advice on how to get Alana?

God help him.

"You're wrong," Alexandra said into the receiver,

her voice shaky enough to snag Sean's attention. "That can't be possible."

Sean shifted in his seat, wishing suddenly that he hadn't come in. He'd really wanted to talk to Hannah but discovered she was out of town, and now he was getting the feeling that this wasn't a conversation he should be hearing.

Another line rang but Alexandra ignored it. She just stared off into space. "No, Mitch, of course not. Then I hope *you* understand that I can't drop it. I *won't* drop the search. If you can't help me, I'll find someone else who will."

She paused, presumably to listen, and then said, "The hell with the FBI."

Sean squirmed some more. He started to get up to leave, but she motioned him back down.

"I know," she said, sighing. "I understand. But anything you can find…anything. Maybe I should meet you in Portland." She picked up a pen and scribbled notes on a pad of paper. "I don't know. I feel so helpless."

After a minute of listening, her shoulders sagged and she sank deeper into her chair. "I know you have, Mitch." She leaned her head back and closed her eyes. "I'll wait to hear from you."

She smiled briefly at whatever this Mitch guy said and then hung up. It took a few moments before she looked up at Sean. "Sorry."

He shrugged helplessly. Granted, he didn't know Alexandra well, but he'd never seen her look so anxious, edgy. "This isn't important. I could've left."

"No, that's okay. I hired a private detective to do some checking on someone who's in a bit of a jam. He says he's hit a brick wall, but he'll keep digging. No big deal."

Right. Man, he hoped she never played poker. Maybe he ought to make an excuse and leave anyway. She was obviously distracted.

The smile she directed his way didn't lessen the strain around her mouth and eyes. "What can I do for you, Sean?"

"Well..." He rubbed the back of his neck, feeling foolish again. "It's about Alana."

"Is she all right?"

"Oh, yeah, she's fine. Great, actually."

Alexandra frowned, then recognition flared in her green eyes.

"I should probably come back." He got to his feet.

"Sit," she commanded with such authority that he did. "I need the distraction."

"What about you?" he asked. "Everything okay?"

"Don't try and change the subject."

"I'm not. Seriously, I'm not prying, but if there's anything I can do..."

She shook her head. "Thanks. All I can do is wait."

He rubbed his jaw, thought for a moment. If the FBI was involved, this was hardly a minor matter. Still, it was none of his business. "Just remember that if you need anything, I have lots of time on my hands these days."

"Oh, my God." She briefly cupped her mouth with her hand. "I haven't even asked about you." Her gaze went to the remnants of the scrape on his mostly healed forehead. "Have you regained your memory?"

"Most of it." He frowned. "I think."

She laughed. "Sorry. I didn't mean to make light of it."

"I was teasing. I wanted to make you laugh."

"Thanks." She gave him a warm smile. "Alana's a lucky lady."

Sean straightened. "Is there something I don't know about?"

"Isn't that why you're here? You said it's about Alana, right? I'd guess you're looking for some advice on how to, let's say, get in her good graces."

He shifted uncomfortably. "Why would you think that?"

"Well…" She was obviously trying to hold back a grin. "Let's see…first, I've seen the way you look at her. Second, Alana is a tough nut to crack. And third, when have you ever come to the office just to chitchat, not to mention looking so sheepish. How am I doing?"

"And I thought *you'd* be a lousy poker player," he muttered.

Her eyebrows rose. "What?"

"Never mind." None of his business, he reminded himself, and then opened his big mouth. "That phone call was no big deal, huh?"

Her expression fell.

"I didn't mean to bum you out. That was my inept way of telling you I want to help."

"It's okay. Really." She pressed her lips together

and stared out the window. Then her cautious gaze met his. "Tell you what. We'll exchange secrets."

He didn't like the sound of that. "Secrets?"

"Okay, so you're an open book. What you have to tell me isn't really a secret."

Sean grunted. "Thanks."

"Seriously, are you in? Whatever we discuss stays here." Her tone and expression were stone-cold sober.

"I'm in."

She nodded and breathed what sounded like relief. "You want to go first?"

"Hell, you already know my problem."

"True." She hesitated. "You're going to think I'm crazy. Hannah and Katherine already do. So does Mitch Barnes, probably, unless he knows something he's not telling me." Her thoughts seemed to wander off again.

"This doesn't sound like much of a secret. Everyone knows about it."

She turned back to him, a blank look in her eyes, and then she sighed. "Well, obviously Mitch has to know—he's the detective I hired. And as far as the other two, they're my best friends, and they still think I'm crazy. But they're loosely involved, so they can't be objective." She looked him meaningfully in the eyes. "You can."

"I'll do my best."

"Okay." She spread her hands on her desk. "Did you want some coffee?"

He shook his head.

"Okay," she began again, "I met this homeless

man last fall. He was hanging around the neighborhood. I'd never seen him before, but something about him seemed familiar, like we had some kind of connection. You know what I mean?''

''Yeah.'' He almost laughed. Man, did he know.

''I'm pretty sure he feels the same way. He's very protective of me and seems to know things about me he really shouldn't know. Little things like my favorite color, foods I like, childhood nursery rhymes I loved to listen to over and over again—'' She made a face. ''I know it sounds crazy, and right now you're probably thinking so what, those could all be lucky guesses. But I feel it here.'' She put a hand to her belly. ''I can't explain it.''

''Then go with your gut. Don't worry about what anyone else thinks.''

She smiled. ''Simple, isn't it?''

''If it were, we wouldn't be having this conversation.''

''Just in case I haven't convinced you I'm crazy, there's one more thing.'' Her hands balled into fists. ''I think he's my father.''

Sean frowned, trying to remember. He'd read something about the scandal in the newspaper when Katherine's father, Louis Kinard, was released from prison. ''Didn't he die in that fire over twenty years ago?''

Slowly she nodded, her eyes watchful, as if she expected him to start laughing at any moment.

''But people would recognize him,'' he said.

''I think he's had plastic surgery. He's got tiny scars

on his face. You have to get up close, but they're there.''

''Wow!'' He wasn't sure what to say. ''Well, if the FBI is involved, something's obviously fishy.''

''That's my point.''

''A no-brainer, as far as I can tell. I'd go for it.''

She gave him a curious look. ''You seem to be re-membering a lot. Have you seen the doctor lately?''

''Last week.'' He shrugged. ''Bits and pieces are still sketchy.''

She knew he was lying, that he had regained all of his memory. He could see it in her eyes. But all she said was, ''Tell me what's happening with you and Alana.''

Just like the old saying, ''out of the frying pan and into the fire.'' ''Okay, first off, I'm not trying to get information about her ex-husband, but I pretty much figured out he has something to do with her throwing up walls like she does.''

One of Alexandra's eyebrows arched. ''She's had a rough time.''

''I know, but that's the past. I'm not her ex.'' Al-exandra looked as if she were about to speak, but thought better of it. ''What? I'm a big boy. I can take it.''

''That's part of the problem. You are young.''

He laughed humorlessly. ''I'm twenty-nine. Christ. I own my own business.''

''I know. I'm only twenty-six, but you've got to realize that Alana has a kid and her own vet practice and she's going it alone. It can't be easy for—''

"Did she say I was too young for her?" Hell, talking to Alexandra wasn't much different from talking to Alana. Why did everyone assume he couldn't handle a relationship or children? He was ready, damn it. He had been for the past year.

"No, she's never mentioned you specifically. I don't even know her all that well. At least, not like Hannah does." She paused. "The only thing more I'll say is that from what I understand, maturity and a sense of responsibility were not her ex-husband's strong suit."

"I'm not him."

"You don't have to convince me of that. Look, if you two got together, there wouldn't be anyone more thrilled than me. But you'll have to take it slow. Show her how serious and responsible you are. I've seen you with Corey. You're good for both of them."

"Thanks." The conversation really hadn't gotten him anywhere. Basically, he'd been told to be patient. Well, hell, that wasn't one of his best traits. Not when it came to Alana.

"I know I haven't been any help, but this is a little tricky. I really can't discuss Alana's—"

"No, of course not. I wasn't asking you to betray any confidences." Frustrated and a little embarrassed, he stood. "I shouldn't have come. It was stupid."

"Please, Sean, don't feel that way." Alexandra stood, too. "I'm rooting for you guys. Big time. I wish I could say more. Just don't give up."

"You, too."

She grinned. "Not a chance."

"Same here." He was definitely in this for the long haul. In fact, he planned on sticking around for so long, she'd think he was part of the damn fixtures.

"DARN IT." ALANA DOVE FOR Felix. Her fingers brushed his fur and she almost got a grip of the ferret's tail, but he slipped between the sofa and the end table. By the time she got to the narrow escape route, he'd disappeared.

She sank onto the sofa and let her head fall back to rest against the wall. What the heck was the matter with her? Why couldn't she concentrate? Why couldn't she manage to carry one small ferret from the clinic to the house without losing him?

Damn.

Sighing, she closed her eyes and rubbed her aching temple. This was all Sean's fault. He was crazy, certifiable, and he'd lured her into his madness. Although they hadn't agreed to pretend to be married, they were basically playing house. Eating meals together, going on family outings, discussing whether it was worth fixing the television or more feasible to buy a new one.

They did just about everything a married couple would do together. Everything but the sex part. And to her horror, she was thinking about it more and more. Yet how could any rational, mature adult consider something so absurd? They had a great relationship, and Corey adored Sean. The odds were, sex would ruin everything.

Yet it seemed as if she could think of little else. Her

ability to concentrate was next to nil. That's why she'd lost Felix.

"Damn it."

"I take it all's not well in paradise." At the sound of Sean's voice, her eyes flew open. "I thought you were helping Cindy."

"I was, but we're through with cleaning out the cages and she didn't have anything else for me to do." He sat down beside her. "What's wrong?"

"I lost Felix."

"You're kidding."

"Do I look like I am?" She sat up straighter and shot him a sarcastic glance. Mostly to disguise the way her hand shook slightly, how her pulse had picked up speed as soon as his thigh brushed hers.

"Wasn't he on a leash?"

"Yes."

At her crisp tone he looked as if he wanted to laugh. "Any idea where he went?"

"That way." She pointed. "But no telling where he is now."

"You know, you might not find him for a day or two."

"I'm well aware of that fact, thank you." She frowned at him. Few people knew about ferrets and how they could burrow into the tiniest of places and not surface until they were hungry.

"I'll help you look." He shrugged. "We could get lucky."

"What do you know about ferrets?"

His brow creased in thought. "When my dad was

stationed in South Carolina, one of the kids in my class had two of the ornery little critters. They'd get out of the cage or slip out of their leashes and disappear, and Jamie's mother would be squealing for days.''

He gave her one of his incredible smiles. She stared at him, her already jumbled thoughts going haywire. "You remember."

"Huh?" His smile disappeared as quickly as Felix had.

"You remembered your friend Jamie and that your dad was in the service and even that you lived in South Carolina."

"Oh. Yeah." The most peculiar look crossed his face and he exhaled sharply. He didn't look at all happy.

"Are you remembering something else?"

He looked like a lost puppy. "It's all fuzzy. Confusing. I told you something about my father just now?"

Was he joking? Had he already forgotten? She studied him closely. He looked earnest enough. "You said your dad was stationed in South Carolina."

He stared off toward the picture window overlooking the emerald-green front lawn, which he'd mowed this morning. "South Carolina."

She stayed silent, letting him contemplate any emerging memories, while she watched confusion and fear trail across his face. No, it wasn't fear exactly, more like desperation or panic. As if he were trying hard to remember but couldn't. Her heart ached for him.

Suddenly he jumped up, startling her. "I saw him."

"Who?"

"Felix."

"What?" She shook her head in disbelief. Sean was finally making headway, grasping wisps of memory, and he was worried about the ferret. "Don't—"

"There he goes." Sean took a dive, nearly knocking over the newly potted Boston fern she had placed on the coffee table yesterday.

"Sean, forget it. Felix will show up when he's hungry."

"I think he squeezed in between the entertainment center and the wall."

Getting up, she walked over and stood beside him. "Well, it's too heavy to move. The television alone weighs a ton. It's older than dirt."

She looked at the CD player on the right. Her dad's old phonograph sat below it, useless at this point, but she couldn't seem to part with it. Beside it was a stack of albums, half of them too warped to play. Corey's videos and CDs occupied the rest of the shelves. The unit really was quite a mess.

"We shouldn't move it anyway. If we did, Felix would just run off." Sean tried to rock the solid oak unit. "Sturdy sucker. You must have had this for a while. They don't make them like this anymore."

"It belonged to my in-laws." She smiled wryly. "My ex-in-laws."

"You get along with them?"

"Better than I do with their son."

Sean chuckled. "Brad's loss, as far as I'm concerned."

"You remembered his name?"

Sean blinked. "I must have overheard you talking to him on the phone."

"Yeah, but you wouldn't know enough to put two and two together unless you remembered something."

"Maybe you said something about him to Hannah or Cindy and I heard."

Alana frowned. She was quite sure she hadn't discussed her ex-husband with anyone lately, and certainly not with Sean around, or Corey, for that matter. She stared at Sean as he busied himself trying to peer behind the unit. The idea that he might not want to remember started to take hold in her mind.

He made a sudden dash toward the hall.

"Did you see Felix?" She hurried after him.

"I think so." He stopped at the bathroom door and flipped on the light.

"I hope he's not in here." She squeezed in beside him and checked out the toilet first. No Felix.

Ferrets could get into just about anything, even spaces only two inches wide, and they usually got out just as easily. But toilets were different. Too many stories with tragic endings. "Did you actually *see* him come in here?" she asked, ready to slip inside and close the door.

"No, he could have made it to the end of the hall." He inclined his head toward her bedroom.

She sighed. Felix would have a field day in there. Not only was the place untidy, but there were numerous nooks and crannies where the little devil would love to hide. She really should have ferretproofed the house by now. The clinic was done, of course, but she hadn't had time to tackle the house yet.

"Tell you what," Sean said. "Why don't I look around in here while you go check out your room?"

"Okay…" She hesitated. "He could be almost anywhere. He might've even crawled up a pipe."

"I know." He gave her a reassuring smile and then took her by the shoulders and turned her toward her room. "Go ahead. I'll search carefully."

She wasn't concerned about that. She was more concerned about the way her body had reacted to his touch, how her knees had gotten soft and her nipples tight. About how much she wanted him to touch her again.

Good thing one of them had more sense than that. Too bad it wasn't her.

She carefully avoided looking at him before heading down the hall. The truth was, as long as she knew Felix hadn't dived into one of the toilets, she wasn't overly worried about locating him. As soon as Corey got home in a couple of hours, he'd make enough racket and turn over enough cushions and everything else to stir the dead. Having Felix loose was more a nuisance than anything.

When she reached the door of her room, she stared in dismay.

What a day for her not to have made her bed.

Leaving the door ajar behind her, she slipped inside, hoping Sean hadn't gotten a glimpse of the mess. After checking the attached bathroom first, and lowering the toilet lid, she pulled the comforter over the bed, fluffed the pillows and placed Jack and Jill, her favorite teddy bears, at their post between the pillows.

She returned to the bathroom for a more thorough search of the linen closet, cabinet and tub, and when she was reasonably certain he wasn't hiding in there, she went back to straighten the bedroom. Thank goodness she hadn't left any clothes lying around.

"Alana?"

Sean stood tentatively at the door.

"Did you find him?" she asked.

"May I come in?"

"Well, sure, but wouldn't it be better if we split up and looked for him?"

Sean's answer was to step inside and glance around. "Nice. You obviously like purple."

"Why would you say that?" She laughed, trying to shake the tension building in her chest and the back of her neck. "Actually, the wallpaper and bedspread are cream and lilac."

"What about the throw pillows?"

"Definitely violet."

"I see." He moved closer, making her stomach flutter.

"Now, what about Felix?" she asked in her most professional voice.

"And the sheets?"

"Pardon?"

"What color are the sheets, Alana?" he asked, his voice low and husky as he moved closer.

"They're—" Her voice broke and she cleared her throat. "We need to go back to the living room. I bet he's still in there. You probably just thought you saw him. It could have been a shadow or anything. Ferrets are very sly—"

He smiled at her nervous babbling.

"Sean, please, we need to go back to the living room."

His gaze locked on hers. "Is that what you want?"

She broke eye contact. She didn't need to ask, she knew exactly what he meant. "I don't know."

"Then trust me."

Her breath caught when he closed the door behind him, and then moved toward her.

CHAPTER THIRTEEN

ALANA FELT AS IF SHE were fifteen again, anticipating her first date. Clammy palms, racing heart, the confidence of a gnat. Except she wasn't a shy, jittery teenager anymore, and the truth was she wanted him. She wanted to taste him, to feel his hot mouth on her skin.

She moistened her suddenly parched lips. "Corey will be—"

"Not coming home for an hour and a half," Sean finished for her.

"Oh. Right."

He stopped several feet away, "Alana?"

It was wrong to want him this much, she thought, forcing her gaze up to meet his. He was still recovering, and she knew nothing could develop between them. He was too young, unsettled. She had Corey to think about.

Sean's quiet laughter broke through her thoughts. "I'd give just about anything to know what's going on in that pretty head of yours."

She gave him a patronizing look. At least she hoped it was. Anything to break the spell. Cut through the web of longing that insulated her from good sense.

He took hold of her hand and tugged her toward him. "Do something for me," he whispered.

At the way his eyes darkened, her heart fluttered and her breasts tingled. She stared at his mouth, the generous fullness of his lower lip, and swallowed hard. "What?"

"Tell me you don't want me."

She tried to yank her hand away.

"Tell me you don't want me, and I'll walk out that door right now."

"This isn't fair."

"Tough."

That startled a laugh out of her. "I'm serious. It's not a matter of a simple physical craving."

One side of his mouth lifted. "Physical craving, huh? Interesting way of putting it."

"See, you're not being serious."

He slid both arms around her. "Sweetheart, I am so serious, you have no idea…"

She smiled at his bittersweet words. They were a good reminder of why she had to keep her distance. Sean was still a kid in some ways. But of course all men were to varying degrees. It was up to her to…

He kissed her. Gently at first. Brushing his lips across hers, lightly, temptingly, and then teasing her lips apart and probing her with his tongue.

Silently she cursed herself for her eagerness, for not even putting up a token struggle. And then she dove in, kissing him back with so much enthusiasm that they both fell onto the bed. An undignified noise rose from her throat and she tried to sit up.

"Don't you believe in fate, Alana?" Sean smiled and turned onto his back, taking her with him.

"But this is happening too fast. We hardly know each other. We—"

He winced, grunted and then shifted beneath her.

"What's wrong?" Oh, God, she was too heavy for him. She tried to roll off him but he wouldn't let her.

Chuckling, he moved his hips, and reached between them to adjust his fly. "Only a minor alteration needed if we ever hope to have more children."

She blinked at him. "My God, Sean, you still believe we're married."

"Relax, I know better." Oddly, he looked sheepish. "Maybe that slip was just wishful thinking."

She didn't know what to say to that admission. Not that she believed it. Nor did she think he was being deceitful. His failed memory made him vulnerable and afraid. He wanted to cling to her because she'd become familiar.

"I've frightened you," he said, regret replacing the desire in his eyes.

"No. But I am beginning to wise up, and it's a little too difficult to talk like this." She tried to get up but he crushed her to him and pushed her onto her back, trapping her with his weight. Nothing scary. She knew if she protested he'd let her go.

"Then no talking," he whispered as his mouth descended on hers.

She obeyed, opening up to him, touching her tongue to his, and then brazenly exploring his mouth.

He responded eagerly, greedily, and slid his hand under her shirt, running his palms over her rib cage and slipping the tips of his fingers under her bra.

Alana held her breath. It had been so long since she'd enjoyed a man's touch. Except this wasn't any man. This was Sean. Who thought she was pretty and smart and made her laugh, who played patiently with Corey, and who'd never asked for a single thing of her. Except for a chance.

She squeezed her eyes shut when his fingers brushed the underside of her breast, then pushed the bra cup up and touched her nipple. She trembled with pleasure, her knees weakening, and the temptation to pull off their clothes greater than she thought possible.

Sean dipped his head, and before she realized what was happening, he put his mouth on her. His tongue swirled around her beaded nipple and she grasped his shoulders for balance. He suckled her and she bit down hard on her lower lip to keep from crying out. When he retreated, she nearly forced his head back to her breast.

"Alana," he whispered hoarsely. "Show me what color your sheets are."

She slowly opened her eyes to the raw desire in his. Her breath caught and nothing came out of her mouth.

He apparently took her silence as consent and started to lift her shirt. "Sean, I don't think—"

"Excellent. Don't think." Pulling her shirt up to her breasts, he pressed a kiss on her belly.

Her reaction was swift and embarrassing. Goose bumps sprang up and she started to go into meltdown.

He pulled back to look at her. "Alana, I want to make love with you."

"I know." The words barely made it out.

He smiled. "That's not quite the response I was looking for."

"I know."

With a chuckle he pulled her close again. "What do you say we take off our clothes?" he whispered, coaxing her with his darkened eyes, running his palm up her shirt and stroking her back.

She glanced at the nightstand clock and tentatively put a hand on his shoulder. Her shirt had bunched up above her waist and she reached down to adjust it.

"Don't," he said.

"Sean, we shouldn't do this. You aren't well."

"Yes, I am." He nuzzled the side of her neck, and worked his way down to her shoulder.

"If you were, you'd have gone back to work."

"But then you'd make me go back to my apartment."

Probably true, but she hated to think about that eventuality. She'd miss him like crazy. But it was difficult to think about anything right now. His hand on her breast felt so damn good, and his mouth... Oh, my... "We have that 'not being serious' problem again."

"I'm very serious," he said, and unfastened her slacks.

She closed her eyes. His mouth found hers and all reason fled. Her entire body was magnetized to him, like a flower seeking the sun.

He unbuttoned her shirt and slipped it off one shoulder and then the other. She cooperated by lifting slightly off the bed, as much as she could anyway, considering that she felt like a sea of jelly. His practiced fingers unhooked the back of her bra quicker than she could have done herself, and in an instant he'd flung it aside.

Drawing back, he gazed down at her, and the humble look in his eyes made her want to cry. No one had ever looked at her like that before. Her breasts were far from perfect, especially after having a child, but she'd never know it by Sean. He cupped the weight of one breast and kissed the tip gently.

His heat became her own as he suckled her harder, his fingers manipulating the zipper to her slacks. And then he stopped suddenly, making her tense.

"Alana," he murmured. "I'm going to go lock the door, and then we're going to finish getting naked and—"

She giggled.

Sean looked at her, his lips curving. "What?"

"Nothing."

"Come on."

She shrugged. "The whole 'getting naked' thing just sounded funny."

"Why?"

"I don't know."

"Trying to give me a complex, are you?"

"Of course not," she protested, before realizing he was teasing. "With a head your size, you think I could give you a complex?"

"You think I have a swelled head?" He grabbed her foot and pulled off her shoe.

"What are you doing?"

The sock came off in spite of her kicking.

When he gripped her ankle, she knew what was coming next. "Sean…" Her voice caught on a giggle as he dragged the tips of his fingers up the soles of her foot.

"What's that again?" He raised his eyebrows in challenge. "I couldn't quite catch it with that silly giggling."

"You turkey—" He did it again, and she almost hurt herself trying not to laugh.

"Give up?" he asked, lowering his hand but keeping it close enough to her foot to be a threat.

"Yes."

"Sure?"

"Yes, damn it." She sank back into the pillows, and then smiled smugly when he dropped her ankle and followed her.

"You're a sly little devil," he said, stretching out beside her, one leg casually thrown over hers.

"Yeah, that's me."

"Stay right here." He went to the door and locked it. "Damn." He shook his head, looked over his shoulder at her. "I'll be right back. Don't move."

She guessed he had gone to get a condom. With Brad, there had been no laughing and talking. It was down to business right out of the gate. Wham bam, thank you ma'am, as the saying went. Sean made her smile and laugh and, heck, he made her giggle, for goodness' sakes.

The door opened and Sean ducked in, packet in his

hand, which he set on the nightstand. "I hope you didn't start without me."

It took a second for his words to sink in. "Sean." Her admonishment fell short when she started laughing.

He grinned and pulled off his T-shirt.

God, he had the best chest...a smattering of hair, but mostly smooth, with nicely defined muscles she was itching to touch.

He pulled off his belt and undid the button of his jeans. "I never did find out what color those sheets are."

She swallowed. Time for her participation. She climbed off the bed and drew down the spread, wishing she could just lie there and watch him undress.

"Ah, lilac. I like surprises."

Before she could respond to his wisecrack, he slipped up behind her and wrapped his arms around her waist. His erection nudged her bottom, and he nuzzled her neck with his moist lips while his hands ran down her breasts and belly.

His abdomen was so flat and firm, whereas hers still had the slight roundness she'd never lost after Corey's birth. But Sean didn't seem to care. His hands lovingly roamed her body as if she was something precious and rare, and his breathing was so ragged she knew it wasn't an act.

She reached behind as far as she could to touch him then, frustrated, turned around in his arms. Her nipples grazed his chest. The sensation was so incredibly erotic it made her dizzy, and she clutched his shoulders.

"Kiss me," he whispered.

She lifted her chin. He was only a breath away, but he waited for her to make the final move.

The symbolic surrender seemed to arouse him further. He quickly finished unfastening her slacks, releasing the zipper and sliding the pants down her legs, stooping to free the garment while kissing her bare thighs.

She never let go of his shoulders, fearing she'd end up a heap on the floor. He surprised her by sliding down her boring white panties, and she automatically tensed.

"Relax," he said, gazing up at her from his crouched position. "We won't do anything you don't want to do."

She should have been embarrassed or flustered or even a little afraid. But she wasn't. Not with Sean.

"Your turn," she said, indicating his jeans with a pointed gaze.

"In a minute." He rubbed his chest against her breasts while he cupped her behind. His eyes drifted closed, a soft moan coming from deep in his throat. "Baby, you feel so good. So smooth and soft. So right."

"Sean, please." She tugged at his pants, tried to pull down the zipper to his fly. But she was all thumbs.

He gave her a brief, hard kiss, then finished the task himself. As soon as he kicked aside his jeans, she let her gaze slide down below his waist.

Boxers. Red ones, too. She smiled. Next to purple, red was her favorite color.

In a flash he was rid of them, and she took a deep breath at the sight of his naked erection. More than a little excited, she would guess. Another giggle threatened the back of her throat. She started mentally counting backward.

"Alana?"

Her eyes had drifted closed and she languidly lifted her lids. His gaze was so dark, goose bumps surfaced on her skin. He said nothing more but guided her to the bed, carefully arranging a pillow before he laid her down.

"I want to be tender yet I want to ravage you," he whispered. "Any preference?"

"I want it all," she whispered back.

The smile slipped away as his gaze roamed her face, then he hungrily took her mouth with his.

She moved over, giving him room to climb in beside her. He crawled in without taking his mouth off hers, one hand splayed across her belly. Instead of lying down, he reclined beside her, his head propped up on one hand, while his other toyed with the soft curls at the juncture of her thighs.

Finally he broke the kiss, and she breathed in deeply, only to have her breath stall in her chest when he caught a nipple between his teeth.

She whimpered, her body jerking.

His head drew back. "I didn't hurt you, did I?"

"No." She tried to swallow. Her mouth was too dry. "It feels good."

He kissed her gently on the lips and then returned to her breasts, where he took turns laving each nipple with his eager tongue.

She wanted to touch him, too, but her right arm was trapped between their bodies. With her free hand she ran her palm over his hip. He shifted to give her better access, and her fingers met tight silky curls. She froze, wanting to explore further yet tempted to pull away.

He must have sensed her indecision because he guided her hand to the brass ring.

She breathed in deeply and slowly allowed her curiosity free rein. Her touch started out gentle, but her impatience got the better of her. She wrapped her hand around him.

"Alana, wait." Sean leaned back, his voice hoarse, his breathing ragged.

"Wait?" She increased the pressure.

"Oh, baby. I'm serious," he said, but made no move to stop her.

"So am I," she whispered, and touched the tip of her tongue to his rock hard nipple.

With a groan, he lay back, his arms falling to his side.

She smiled victoriously.

He eyed her with undisguised amusement. "Think you're pretty hot stuff, don't you?"

Before she could object, he had her on her back, her arms pinned down as he hovered over her.

"Hey…" she said lamely, and then gave in to his kiss. More intense this time. Incredibly, even more exciting.

He reached for the foil packet he'd left on the night-stand. "I wish we had all day and night, Alana," he said with regret as he tore open the packet.

She nodded, willing him to hurry.

Once he'd sheathed himself, he spread her legs. As he slowly slid into her, Alana heard him murmur something about coming home.

CHAPTER FOURTEEN

SEAN WAITED UNTIL HE heard Alana say good-night to Corey and then head for her room before he slipped out of his. He loved that kid, but of all nights for him to want to stay up late to watch some *National Geographic* special.

If a television program was educational, Alana usually relented and let him stay up past his eight-thirty bedtime. It was already nine-forty, and Sean's patience was running a little thin.

Dinner had been sheer torture. Sitting in his usual seat across the table from her, pretending they hadn't just had the most incredible afternoon in history was more than he could take.

He looked down at his fly. The sucker hadn't gone down all night. It seemed everything Alana did had looked sexy. The way she'd cut up vegetables for the salad and buttered Corey's roll. Hell, even the way she'd washed dishes while Sean dried.

Damn, but he had it bad.

She was going to flip out when he told her he loved her. But he did. And then again, maybe she wouldn't freak. Maybe she felt the same way he did. So why had she avoided eye contact at dinner? And tried to chase him out of the kitchen when she cleared the table? He knew he should be patient, but since this afternoon...

He stopped at her door, took a quick look over his shoulder to make sure Corey hadn't left his room to go to the bathroom, and then knocked softly. After waiting nearly a minute, he knocked again.

The door opened slowly. Alana poked her head out. It looked as if she already had on her robe. "Hi."

"Hi yourself." He touched the tip of her nose. "Can I come in? The coast is clear."

She hesitated, ducking her head to look past him toward Corey's room. "Okay, but only for a minute."

He didn't like the sound of that. But he kept his mouth shut until he got inside and closed the door quietly behind him. "What's wrong?"

"Nothing."

"Alana." He reached out to touch her cheek but she moved out of the way. "Yeah, right."

"Nothing is wrong," she insisted, pulling the sash of her pink robe tighter, emphasizing her slim waist.

Hard to believe she'd already had a child. Her breasts and tummy were nice and firm, without compromising her feminine softness. Hell, he was getting turned on just thinking about it.

"What did you want, Sean?"

"Not the cold shoulder, that's for sure."

Her expression softened. "This afternoon was—" She moistened her lips. "This afternoon was truly wonderful. Frankly, I've never experienced anything like it." Blushing, she picked at a thread from the sash. "But it hasn't changed anything."

"Right."

She looked up, the regret in her eyes burning a hole in his gut. "Okay, you're right. There is something wrong. Me. I was wrong in giving in this afternoon."

"Giving in? You're telling me you weren't as aroused as I was? I don't remember doing much co-ercing."

She started to reach for him, then quickly lowered her hand. "No, that's not what I meant. I was a full participant. I wanted you. I wanted everything. But that's the problem. I feel horribly guilty."

"Why? You're legally divorced. I'm unattached."

"But I'm thinking clearly and you aren't." Her shoulders sagged. "Or at least I'm supposed to be."

He relaxed, discovering this was not such a big ob-stacle. "And why is it that I can't think for myself?"

His teasing tone didn't soothe her. She looked so miserable he wanted to pull her into his arms.

Gently he took her by the elbow. "Do we have to stand at the door?"

Her gaze darted to the bed, and she slowly nodded. "But all we're doing is talking."

"You got it."

There were no chairs, so she sat on the edge of the bed near the pillows, overlapping her robe so her legs wouldn't show. Sean purposely left a couple feet be-tween them. Being patient was going to kill him.

"Corey's asleep?" he asked, trying to relax her.

"As soon as his head hit the pillow."

"His eyes were drooping during the last commercial."

"I know." She sighed. "Of all nights for *National Geographic* to have a special."

Hope buoyed his spirits.

"Only so we could talk," she added quickly.

He nodded hope not yet lost. "I know."

The silky material of her robe slipped and exposed one smooth leg. She didn't seem to notice, and he almost wished she'd cover up again. Save him from temptation. Summoning all his willpower, he resisted the urge to stroke her satiny skin. There'd be time later.

"I'm going to be totally honest," he said, surprised when he saw fear flicker in her eyes. "I want to kiss you right now. But I'll keep my hands to myself until we get this sorted out. Until I convince you that you have nothing to feel guilty about."

She didn't seem particularly pleased.

"But then again, one quick kiss wouldn't hurt."

A grin tugged at her lips. "You're incorrigible."

"I try my best."

Any hint of a smile disappeared and she groaned. "Sean, darn it, this isn't helping."

"What?"

She made a move to get up, but he snagged her by the wrist and pulled her toward him. "You wanted to talk."

"What I want is to erase what happened this afternoon."

That stung. "But you can't."

She must have realized how that sounded, because her expression softened and her gaze went to his forehead. She pushed his hair aside and touched the scraped area. Most of the abrasions were healed. Other than an occasional headache, he hadn't had any pain for nearly a week.

"It looks pretty good," she said softly. "I bet the doctor releases you to go back to work in a couple of days."

"Probably." He took her hand and pressed a kiss into her palm. "Are you going to send me back to my dreary, lonely apartment?"

Her uncensored expression told him she wanted him to stay, and his heart lifted. "Oh, Sean, I've—Corey and I have both enjoyed your company."

He raised his eyebrows.

"Okay, so maybe I've more than enjoyed it," she admitted, blushing. "But it's not that simple."

"Only if you make it difficult." The hell with patience. He kissed the inside of her wrist, then moved further up her arm to her elbow.

"This isn't right, Sean." Her eyes drifted closed. "Please, I feel guilty enough. I should have been stronger." She opened her eyes and tried to twist out of his hold. "You can't even remember who you are. This isn't right."

"I remember," he murmured, his mouth pressed to her arm.

Alana frowned. He'd spoken so softly she couldn't be sure she heard correctly. "What did you say?"

He tried to slip a hand into her robe where the lapels barely overlapped, but she pushed him away.

"Hey." He brought his head up.

"You remember?"

He shrugged, looking a little sheepish. "Yeah."

She jerked her arm away. "Everything?"

"Alana…" He reached for her, but she got up, evading him just in time.

"What do you remember?"

With a sigh, he fell back heavily onto the bed. "Not everything."

"Then what?"

He glanced over at her, but stared up at the ceiling.

"What do you remember?" she asked again, this time more sternly. How could he have deceived her?

"I remember the accident, or at least part of it."

"And?"

He exhaled loudly. "My name, my family…"

"Your past?"

He shrugged.

"Corey and me?"

He didn't answer.

"So basically, everything."

"No, not really."

Anger built inside of her. He looked guilty. It wasn't her imagination. He even seemed to be avoiding eye contact. "When did you start remembering?"

Reluctantly he met her gaze. "Um, I'm not sure. Yesterday, I think."

"You think?"

"Come on, Alana, what does it matter?" He

reached for her again but she moved away from the bed.

"You have to ask?" She had a good mind to throw a pillow at him. He suddenly looked so damn innocent. Or at least tried to. She knew better.

"Would you please come here so we can talk about it?" He patted a spot on the bed beside him.

She ignored the request, afraid she might lash out at him. "All right," she said calmly, "I'll give you the benefit of the doubt. Assuming your memory returned yesterday, when were you planning on telling me?"

He looked sheepish again. "Today. In fact, I—"

She cut in, not wanting to hear any more lies. "Just not before we made love. Oh, excuse me. Had sex."

Anger flickered in his face. "You want to explain that?"

"You know damn well what I mean."

He stared at her for a long, agonizing moment, disappointment written all over his face. "You know better. We did make love." Hurt gave way to anger in his eyes. "Unless you considered that a pity screw."

She reared her head back, startled at his words.

"You know, give the poor guy a bone. He's messed up in the head, can't work, can't do anything—"

"Do you have any idea how tempted I am to slap your face?"

"Yeah?" He grunted with disgust. "How do you think I felt when you said we had sex?"

She wrapped her arms around herself. "Point taken."

Sean smiled sadly. "You're trying to push me away, but it won't work."

Alana shook her head. She hadn't pushed him away. In fact, she'd let him get too close. "You're wrong. Not that it matters."

"Why aren't you willing to listen? I told you I was well. Hell, I even admitted I hadn't said anything because you would have sent me packing."

Vaguely she recalled their whispered conversation. "That didn't count," she said lamely.

"Why? Because you were too turned on to hear me?"

Jerk. "Because it sounded as if you were teasing."

"Right."

She bristled at his patronizing tone. He had no right putting her on the defensive. "Good." She tried not to sound smug. "I'm glad you've regained your memory. Now that you have, tell me about Brenda."

He shrugged. "What do you want to know?"

She hadn't expected him to be so nonchalant. In fact, she'd expected him to suddenly have selective memory. "You do remember her, right?"

"Of course. We went out for nearly two years." He frowned. "How do you know about Bren?"

There wasn't an ounce of trepidation in his tone. Just plain curiosity.

"Your neighbor told me about her when I went to your apartment. She also left a message on your answering machine." Alana's cheeks heated when she realized it was obvious she'd listened to his messages.

"I thought maybe any callers could help you in some way."

Sean frowned again. "Why'd she call? I haven't heard from her in a while."

That he seemed so unconcerned annoyed the heck out of Alana. "She wants you to give her another chance," she said bluntly, hoping to give him a jolt.

He drew his head back in surprise, and then he laughed. "Her car again, huh?"

"What?"

"That's why she called."

"She didn't mention a car."

Turning on his side, he propped his head up with his hand. "Have I ever told you what beautiful eyes you have?"

Her budding confusion returned to anger at his callous attitude. "How can you be such a jerk? I had you figured so wrong."

He stared at her, his face darkening as he lifted himself to a sitting position. "Explain."

"That you even need an explanation makes you a bigger jerk," she said, half regretting her words when anger ravaged his face.

But to his credit he stayed calm. He swung his legs over the side of the bed, his hair falling in his eyes. She wanted to rake her fingers through it as she'd done this afternoon, and she felt a flutter between her breasts.

"Obviously you've chosen to think the worst of me. The woman I thought I knew would have given me a chance to defend myself."

She hugged herself, struggling against the temptation to cave in and believe anything he said just to keep the peace. Brad had done this same thing. Tried to shift blame on her. She'd been younger then, weaker, too eager to please, and she'd slipped denial around her like a comfortable cloak. Not any more.

"Okay," she said. "Go ahead."

Sean didn't move, didn't say a word at first. He was obviously still very angry, probably trying to decide if this discussion was worth it. If Alana was worth it. Or maybe he was trying to come up with a reasonable story.

"Yes, Brenda and I had a steady relationship for well over a year. We had fun and I liked her very much. Still do, in fact. But we both agreed the relationship would never go any further. I was ready to settle down and she still wanted to party."

He sounded so matter-of-fact. Had she misjudged him? Feeling a little jittery suddenly, Alana almost sat beside him on the bed. "Did she know how you felt?"

"Of course." His chin jutted in challenge. "Maybe hard for you to believe, but we had a mature, adult conversation about it before we called it quits."

She let his sarcasm roll off. "Judging from her message, I think she may have changed her mind."

He pushed his hair back and laughed. "I guarantee you that call only meant she needs something, probably for me to look at her car or her furnace. Call her back yourself, if you want."

As if she'd do that. "You know, I'm sorry I even brought her up because none of that really matters."

"There you go. I tried to tell you."

"The reason it doesn't matter is because we're only friends. That's all we'll ever be." She saw the hurt in his eyes and briefly looked away. "Sean, there'll be lots of other Brendas, and one of them will want kids, she'll want the same things you do."

"What about you? Don't *we* want the same thing?"

"I already have a son."

He blinked, looking unsure for the first time. "Does that mean you don't want any more children?"

"No it doesn't."

"You've lost me."

Alana tugged on her sash. One more pull and she wouldn't be able to breathe. This was so damn difficult. Why couldn't he understand how different they were? He still had wild oats to sow. She had a child to raise. "How long have you lived here?"

"Longer than you," he said, his tone defensive. "Why?"

"Let's start over. How long have you lived in any one place?"

He narrowed his gaze. "I've been here in Seattle for the past three years."

"During that time, did you go on any vacations?"

"Sure."

"How many?"

He frowned. "I don't know. Three or four."

"Where?"

"What is this about?"

She smiled sadly. "I saw the pictures in your apartment, Sean. Ones of you in Europe, the Caribbean, Hawaii, places I couldn't even recognize.''

"And your point would be?" His expression tightened. He was more than defensive now, he was angry.

"You can't have a family and travel the world, too. You're young. You still have so much to do and see.''

"I've already seen it all. My dad was in the air force. I got sick of moving.''

"Or maybe you got too used to it.''

"I've planted myself here, haven't I? When I do go away, it's to visit my sisters and their kids.''

Alana paused. He did have a point. But still... "You have a lot of freedom to come and go at your age, freedom you'd miss if—''

"For Christ sake, you're acting like there are a couple of decades between us. How old are you?''

"Thirty-two.''

"I'll be thirty next month. Only two friggin' years between us. Big deal.''

"It's different—''

"I'm not done. How old were you when you had Corey?''

She sighed. He didn't understand there was a difference between them. Between most men and women at that age. She'd learned the hard way. "Twenty-six.''

"Ah, I guess you weren't ready to be a mother.''

"Of course I was.''

His eyebrows lifted. "But I'm not ready to settle down at thirty? Go figure.''

"Other than college, I lived in Olympia my entire

life. From the time I was twelve years old I knew I wanted to be a veterinarian. By the time I was twenty-two, I knew I wanted to be a wife and mother. My life has always been very linear. Boring. Typical.''

He laughed humorlessly. "This is rich. You're telling me that you had half your life planned at twelve, but at thirty I can't decide what's right for me. Lady, you are really something.''

Put that way, her argument sounded pretty bad. But he still missed the point. She was cut out to do the family thing. Always had been. Lately she'd realized she'd been wrong to force Brad into that same mold, a mistake she wasn't about to make again.

"I'm obviously explaining this badly,'' she said, wishing the conversation would just end. Wishing they could go back to the way they were.

"That's an understatement. Because you aren't making a damn bit of sense.''

"Please keep your voice down. You'll wake Corey.''

He briefly closed his eyes and pinched the bridge of his nose. "Sorry.''

"I'm not blaming you for anything, Sean. I take full responsibility.'' Granted, he had misled her about regaining his memory, but she decided to let that slide. Enough tension had mounted. "I had no business ruining our friendship with sex. I wasn't thinking.''

"News flash. You still aren't.''

She knew anger and hurt fueled his sarcasm, but she was getting pretty ticked off, too. He wasn't even trying to understand what she was telling him. "Maybe we should talk tomorrow."

"Why? You've already made up your mind about me." Resignation settled into the weary lines around his eyes, and panic squeezed her heart.

"I hope we can still be friends."

"I thought we were, Alana." He sighed. "I really did."

"And I ruined it." She suddenly felt disgustingly close to tears.

"Not with sex, you didn't. Lovers should always be friends first. You're ruining it now."

He headed for the door, and she really started to panic. She didn't want to talk any more tonight, but she didn't want it to end this way, either.

"Sean, wait."

He stopped, but didn't turn around.

"We'll talk tomorrow, okay?"

He stayed silent for several long moments and then slowly turned to look at her. "What's the point? You've already judged me, squeezed me into some nice tidy category you can understand."

"You're not being fair."

"I'll tell you what's not fair—you making me pay the price for your ex-husband's faults."

She gasped. "That is so untrue—"

"Not fair is you thinking I'm too young to handle the responsibility of a family." He started toward her, and she flinched.

"I may be young in your eyes," he said, grabbing

both her arms and drawing her close. "But I'm wise enough to see how good we are together."

Before she could utter a word, before she could even think to protest, he kissed her. His arms around her felt so right...his lips on her lips...

He broke the kiss as abruptly as he started it. "Tell you what, Alana, when you're done painting every man with the same brush as Brad, give me a call."

He released her, and then quietly slipped out the door.

CHAPTER FIFTEEN

ALANA KNEW SEAN HAD left before she saw the empty guest-room closet or noticed that the bed had been made up with fresh linen. She'd hurt him. Of course he wouldn't stick around.

She leaned against the doorframe for support and stared blindly into the room. God, she hadn't wanted them to part company, or if they had to, not like this. Nor had she wanted to stay awake half the night reliving his last kiss. Even the replay tasted so final.

God, what had she done? How was she going to explain to Corey that she'd chased Sean away?

The house already seemed too quiet. At six in the morning it usually was peaceful. But today it was empty, glum. Just like her heart.

If only Sean had listened, if only he'd tried to be objective. She wasn't just trying to spare herself or Corey from getting hurt. Sean was at risk, too. He was a nice, decent guy who'd feel horrible later when he realized he'd made a mistake.

Decent enough that he might even try to stick out the relationship, even if he was miserable.

She forced herself to go inside the room. It still smelled like him, that kind of woodsy, outdoor scent that seemed to cling to him. Or maybe it was just her imagination because she already missed him.

Damn, this was exactly what she'd been trying to avoid. Fine job. She'd screwed up good this time. And not only had she just totally turned her life upside down, but tomorrow she had to face Brad. Such a cheery thought.

She hadn't told Corey yet that his dad was coming. She didn't trust Brad to show up. If a better offer came along, she wouldn't put it past him to stand his son up. He'd done it before.

Why the hell was she thinking about Brad at a time like this?

She sank to the edge of the bed, feeling a little shaky, because Sean was partly right. She did fear getting involved with a man again. Her ability to trust anyone had been shattered. Her experience with Brad had done that to her. She knew that intellectually. But when it came to putting her heart on the line, it wasn't that easy.

Okay, she was a coward. But even that was still her decision, whether she wanted to take that sort of risk or not, and she didn't. Simple.

She covered her face with her hands and groaned. Not simple at all. She'd put herself out there by sleeping with Sean. How could she have been so weak and stupid? They'd had a great relationship, and now they had nothing.

Maybe she was overreacting. Maybe Sean just needed time to cool off and then he'd understand. She was incredibly tired, both mentally and physically worn out. In the short period of time they'd had that afternoon, they'd managed to make love twice, and she was a little achy from previously unused muscles.

Not made love, she reminded herself. Had sex. That's all it was. Lots of people nowadays had relationships based on sex. It allowed them to satisfy a normal, physical need without having to make any declarations. Maybe after this misunderstanding blew over they could...

Who was she kidding? That wasn't her. She didn't believe Sean was that casual about sex, either.

She crawled into the bed and curled up, burying her face into a pillow, hoping to find his scent again. But he'd laundered the linen before he left. Even though he'd been so angry. She shook her head. Of course. She wasn't the least surprised. That was so typically Sean.

That awful gnawing feeling that she got in the pit of her stomach when she knew she'd made an awful mistake started with a vengeance. This time the pain seemed almost physical. She curled up tighter, until she was in a fetal position, but found no relief.

This was crazy. She had to work today. Six appointments had been scheduled for this morning alone. And after she got back from the clinic, she had to start ferretproofing the house. Corey was beginning to bring Felix and Fran in more and more and...

Tears burned the back of her eyes. How the hell was she going to explain Sean's absence to Corey?

She heard him close the bathroom door. Too loudly, as he did most mornings when he first woke up. She glanced at the digital clock as she forced herself up from the bed. Time for her morning routine. Good, really. Keeping busy would keep her from thinking.

Stopping at the mirror, she dabbed at her swollen eyes. Makeup would take care of the dark circles beneath. If Corey asked, she'd tell him she was having another sinus attack.

She took a final look and raked her fingers through her tangled hair, remembering how Sean had done the same thing with his fingers.

Damn, she had to stop. She couldn't afford to think about Sean, or yesterday afternoon.

As she left the guest room, she closed the door. Better wait until this afternoon to break the news to Corey about Sean leaving. Then maybe she could do it without crying.

ALEXANDRA SAT ON the couch and took several deep breaths, not at all sure it would help. She'd been doing deep breathing exercises all morning. Ever since she'd gotten the call from Mitch Barnes.

She stared at the door, continuing to breathe deeply and willing the doorbell to ring. She hoped Hannah showed up first, for moral support if nothing else. And if Alexandra did happen to faint, she'd much rather have Hannah tending to her than a total stranger.

A minute later the doorbell finally chimed, and she froze. She dragged her clammy hands down the front of her jeans and forced herself to stand, then ordered her leaden feet to move.

She looked through the peephole. It was Hannah.

With a mixture of relief and disappointment, Alexandra flung the door open.

Hannah had her spare key out, ready to unlock the door. She looked up, her eyes wide, her face pale. "Jeez, are you okay?"

Alexandra nodded. "I'm sorry I was so cryptic on the phone. I just wanted you here with me this afternoon."

Hannah looked confused, and rightfully so, but she smiled. "All you have to do is ask, and I'm here."

"I know." Alexandra opened the door wider. "Come on, I'll fill you in before he gets here."

"Who?"

"Ernie Brooks."

"Okay." Hannah gave her a concerned look as she made her way to the couch. After she curled up in one corner, she asked, "Who's Ernie Brooks?"

"Remember that private detective I hired to check out Gary Devlin? His name is Mitch Barnes. He works for your friend Dylan Garrett at Finders Keepers."

Hannah nodded and shrugged at the same time. She knew some of what Alexandra had been up to, but Alexandra hadn't told her everything.

"Apparently, Ernie Brooks is another retired FBI agent. I think he may have been Mitch's partner." She went to the kitchen to get them some water but kept talking. "Anyway, Mitch has asked this guy to come talk to me."

"About what? Did they find something out about Gary?"

Alexandra returned and set down the glasses on the

coffee table. "Mitch didn't say anything specifically, but I have to assume they have. Why else would this Ernie Brooks be coming to see me?"

"To tell you to back off again."

"He's *retired* FBI. He doesn't work for Finders Keepers. It has to mean something, Hannah."

"Probably." Hannah's smile was hardly reassuring. "But the news may not be what you want to hear."

"I realize that." Alexandra reclaimed her side of the couch. Deep down, she knew differently. Ernie Brooks was coming to tell her that Gary Devlin was her father, that he hadn't perished in the fire, that he'd been working with the FBI on some case and had to disappear. Situations like that really happened. They weren't just Hollywood fantasies.

Hannah scooted closer and squeezed her hand. "I'm not trying to be a downer. I just don't want you to get your hopes up and then be depressed if you don't get the news you want. You do realize this is a long shot. I mean, it's been over twenty years..."

"I know." Alexandra leaned over and hugged her friend, hoping to chase away the concern in her eyes. Funny how calm she'd become since Hannah had arrived. Talking out loud probably helped. She'd been alone with her crazy thoughts since the call yesterday afternoon. "Whatever happens, I'm glad you're here with me."

"Me, too."

Alexandra sat back and straightened her shirt. "Want some hot tea?"

Hannah immediately got to her feet. "How about I get you some? Nice soothing chamomile ought to—"

The doorbell cut her off.

They both looked at the door and then each other.

"How about you get the door instead?" Alexandra moistened her parched lips. "I don't think I can stand up."

Hannah went to the door, and then glanced back at Alexandra. "Here goes," she said as she swung it open.

The man standing there was close to seventy, not too tall, robust, but fairly nondescript, which had probably made him good at his job. "Alexandra?" He extended his hand to Hannah. "I'm Ernie Brooks."

"I'm her friend Hannah." She stepped to the side. "That's Alexandra," she said with a sweeping hand gesture. "Come in."

"Ah, yes." He gave a slight nod as he approached, almost as if he'd suddenly recognized her, which was impossible. Alexandra had never seen him before.

She forced herself to stand. "Thank you for coming, Mr. Brooks."

"Ernie," he corrected, his palm warm and somehow reassuring as he pressed it to hers.

"Please, have a seat."

He took the leather director's chair on the other side of the coffee table.

"I was just about to get some tea," Hannah said to Ernie. "Would you like a cup?"

"Sure. Thanks." He had a nice smile, and a very pleasant manner about him.

Hannah hesitated for a moment, probably wondering if she should stay in the living room. Alexandra's place was so small, it didn't really matter. She'd hear everything they said in the kitchen.

"I'll be right back," she said, giving Alexandra a private thumbs-up.

Ernie Brooks had been watching Alexandra with shrewd eyes that belied his affable appearance.

"You're nervous," he said, "which I can understand." His expression turned grim. "So I'll be perfectly blunt—I'm afraid I may not have as much information for you as you'd hoped."

Her heart plummeted. "But you came all this way."

He shrugged. "Mitch knew I'd be in the area on vacation, anyway."

Fighting back tears, she shook her head. "Do you have any information for me? Anything at all."

Hannah reappeared without the tea and sat beside Alexandra, quietly taking her hand.

Ernie leaned back, studying Alexandra, his expression completely unreadable.

Why didn't he say something? Alexandra squeezed Hannah's hand. "I mean, it doesn't make sense that you'd come here to tell me the same thing Mitch could tell me on the phone."

"I was here in Seattle the night of the fire," he said finally. "When your father was killed."

When your father was killed. Alexandra's heart thudded. Not, When your father was *supposed* to have been killed. Was he telling her this was it? The end of the road to Finders Keepers's investigation? That Gary Devlin wasn't her father?

"Wait a minute." Alexandra tried to sort out her converging thoughts. "The FBI investigated a house fire?"

He slowly shook his head. "I happened to be in the city on another assignment, which I had just wrapped up, so I was instructed to check out the theft and murder of a priest at a church nearby."

"Our Lady of Mercy," Hannah said, her voice eerily quiet, almost a whisper.

"Yes." Ernie glanced at her.

"A religious relic was stolen that night, a crystal cross, I believe," she said casually, tension radiating from her, and her grip on Alexandra's hand tightening. "Was it ever recovered?"

"Not that I'm aware." Ernie also noticed Hannah's strong reaction, Alexandra noticed. His gaze narrowed, as if he were making a mental note to follow up later.

"Sorry to have interrupted," Hannah said, looking from Ernie to Alexandra. "Debbie North got me interested in the story."

When Ernie didn't immediately continue, Alexandra asked, "What did the theft and murder have to do with the fire?"

"Nothing, as it turned out. But since your family was so prominent and the church happened to be the one you attended, we thought it was worth a shot to investigate the fire."

"But there was no relationship."

He shook his head.

"And Mitch figured if he got someone to come here in person, someone who'd actually been there that night, to tell me I'm crazy and to quit wasting everyone's time, that I'd finally give up."

Compassion gleamed in his eyes but he offered no denial.

Alexandra felt the sting of tears. She'd been so sure today would bring good news. "Did he tell you about the doll?" she asked, her voice breaking. "How could this man have my doll or know so many little details about me?"

Hannah turned sharply toward her. Alexandra hadn't told her friend everything. She'd gotten tired of the looks of pity from her well-meaning friends.

"Mr. Brooks, I'm not trying to be difficult." Alexandra sniffed, praying the floodgates wouldn't burst. "I just want to understand. My God, I just want closure."

Suddenly he looked old and tired. He scrubbed at his eyes and then pushed both hands through his graying brown hair. "Look, I can't talk about that night. I'm not with the Bureau anymore, but I swore an oath that I would never reveal any information learned on a case. Do you understand?"

Miserable and weepy, she nodded.

"Alexandra, look at me."

His voice was stern, and she lifted her gaze to his. He stared at her for what seemed like infinity, his eyes intense and direct, but somehow kind.

"If I knew that your father had walked out of that

fire, I couldn't admit that to you," he said slowly, each word deliberate. "Do you understand?"

She stared back, confused. She didn't understand anything anymore.

"Alexandra," Ernie said, making sure he had her attention. "Even if your father were alive, and I'm certainly not saying that he is, where has he been all these years? Why wouldn't he have contacted you sooner?"

"I was hoping you could tell me that," she said softly, her thoughts a mass of confusion.

He sat back watching her. "Did this man claim he was your father?"

She shook her head, not trusting herself to speak.

"I understand this is an emotional issue, and it's difficult for you to think logically." Ernie exhaled loudly and glanced at Hannah. "I wish I could help you."

Alexandra choked back a sob.

"Honey…" Hannah slid closer and put an arm around her friend's shoulders. "It's okay."

"No, it's not. It's not okay." Alexandra leaned forward, clasping her hands between her knees. "Please, I have another question. If Gary Devlin were my father, you wouldn't tell me, would you?"

A ghost of a smile played at the corners of Ernie's mouth. "No, Alexandra, I couldn't tell you."

She nodded, fresh tears stinging the back of her eyes. Maybe she was being foolish to still hope. She didn't care.

And then he added, "All I can tell you is to follow your heart...kitten."

"What did you say?"

Ernie just stared back at her.

She covered her mouth with her hand. Her father had used that nickname for her. Coincidence? Or was Ernie trying to tell her something?

Or was she going crazy?

"Well, I best be getting on my way." Ernie rose. "Sorry I couldn't help you more."

Alexandra sat frozen, too numb to do or say anything.

"You two take care now, and good luck to you," Ernie said as he walked to the door.

"Thank you," Alexandra finally whispered, the tears starting to gush as she watched him let himself out.

Hannah handed her a box of tissues and she dabbed at her eyes. She had to pull herself together. No way would she give up. She had to go find her father.

"OUCH!"

This was the second time today Sean had clipped his finger with the damn hammer. He never did that. Well, rarely, anyway. Only since he'd been preoccupied with thoughts of Alana.

He shook his head, then cursed under his breath when he realized he'd nailed down the wrong side of the molding and had to rip the whole thing up.

That did it.

He tossed the hammer into his toolbox without securing it properly and picked up the rest of the nails. Definitely time to quit for the day. Before he ended up in a body cast. Hell, he hadn't even gotten the doctor's release yet for the last accident. His insurance company would go ape if he landed in the hospital again.

After loading up his truck, he stopped at the burger joint a block from his apartment and picked up two chili dogs for dinner. Not exactly approved by the Heart Association, but it was either the dogs, or go to bed hungry.

He'd gone the hunger route a couple of nights during the past week. Eating alone was the pits. He'd gotten used to the teasing banter at the Fletcher kitchen table, and listening to Corey enthusiastically describe his antics at the day care, or yammer about how he'd be starting kindergarten this September like all the big kids.

Sean missed watching Alana. The way she rolled her eyes at Corey's exaggerated tales, or let a smile light up her face. He missed talking with her. Deciding together what movie they should rent or what sitcom to watch. If only she weren't so damn stubborn and myopic.

After pulling the truck into a spot near his apartment, he stowed his toolbox on the floor beneath an old towel and grabbed his chili dogs. Once he got inside, he stopped in the kitchen to check the answering machine and caller ID.

Of course she hadn't called. The woman was too damn stubborn for her own good. He grabbed a cola out of the fridge and took his food into the office, where he plopped down in front of his computer.

Too many stacks of blueprints and work orders littered his desk. There wasn't even a spot for his damn dinner. Work had started piling up long before the accident, and now he could hardly keep his head above water. He'd rescheduled most of the jobs, which pretty much had him tied up well into fall.

No getting around it. He was going to have to hire some help. Not just more subcontractors, but permanent payroll employees who'd want sick leave and vacation and health benefits.

The thought gave him a headache. Using subcontractors was so much easier and cheaper. But if he wanted to prove himself as a serious, established contractor, he'd have to expand and start bidding on larger jobs.

It also meant he'd have to stay put in Seattle. That wasn't a problem. He liked it here. If he got antsy, he could take trips to visit his sisters and brother and their kids, just as he'd done the past three years.

So why hadn't he already bitten the bullet? Why hadn't he expanded Everett Construction? The work was there. He needed only to make the commitment.

Had Alana been right about him not being ready to settle down? Could he stay in one place, plant roots?

He muttered a pithy four-letter word he hadn't used in a long time. She had him stupidly second-guessing himself. He hadn't expanded the business yet because it hadn't been the right time. Now it was. End of story.

Dinner had grown cold but he didn't have the energy to go to the kitchen to nuke the chili dogs. They looked disgusting, anyway. He'd gotten used to home-made dinners like meat loaf or roasted chicken with mashed potatoes and fresh green beans. Dinners he and Alana used to cook together.

His gaze was drawn to the phone. If he broke down and called, it would be to speak with Corey. Obviously Alana had already said her piece. Nothing more to discuss with that stubborn woman.

When he'd left last week, he told her she was going to have to call him, tell him she was ready for a re-lationship.

And damn it, he meant it. She had to be the one who made the call. Simple.

He stared glumly at the phone.

Good thing he wasn't holding his breath.

Because it sure as hell wasn't ringing.

CHAPTER SIXTEEN

"MOM, WHY DOESN'T SEAN come to our house anymore?" Corey looked up at Alana with big sad eyes.

She finished washing her hands, then wiped down the sink where she'd just sterilized a scalpel. The clinic was spotless, even the waiting room. But then it should be. She'd spent every spare minute scrubbing.

"He's busy," she said, drying her hands and eyeing the basket of dirty towels in the closet. "He has a lot of work to catch up on after being sick for so long."

"But we haven't seen him for a whole week. You're busy, and I see you."

Maybe she should throw in a load of laundry. Cindy would have a fit. Lately she'd complained she didn't have enough to do around the clinic.

"Doesn't he like me anymore?" Corey mumbled, staring at the toe of his sneakers.

She crouched down in front of him, forgetting about towels and Cindy and everything else. "Of course he does. You know better than that."

He shrugged his narrow shoulders. "Maybe he doesn't like me just like Daddy doesn't."

"Come here." She hugged him to her. "That's not

true.'' She managed to keep her voice gentle…amazing, considering that at the moment, she wanted to inflict major bodily harm on Brad.

The jerk had shown up on Friday, spent fifty minutes with his son and then took off for the airport because Sheila didn't like him spending the night away from home.

Probably because she'd figured out what a two-timing jackass he really was.

Alana lifted Corey's chin and smiled at him. ''Your daddy loves you very much. So does Sean.''

''It doesn't feel like it.''

''Daddy had a plane to catch, honey. Or he would have stayed longer.''

''Not Daddy.'' He bowed his head and studied a crack in the tile floor, tracing it with the toe of his sneaker. ''Sean used to do stuff with us all the time.''

''I know, and we'll see him again soon. He loves going fishing with you, and to the zoo, and…''

She took a steadying breath. That was the truth. She could see the joy in Sean's face when he spent time with her and Corey. But she'd pushed him away. Had she done the same to Brad? Had she been the one who'd pushed him out of their lives?

No, she was being silly. He'd walked away. No encouragement needed.

''Do you think maybe he went on a trip?'' Corey asked. ''He could have gone to Hawaii or something.''

''Hawaii?'' She laughed at the way he pronounced it, grateful for the brief respite. Before her thighs started cramping, she gripped the counter for support and straightened. "How do you know about Hawaii?"

"Sean told me about it. He goes there sometimes."

"Oh." Big surprise. She already knew about Sean's penchant for travel. That was part of the problem, but of course she wouldn't dampen Corey's spirits. "Maybe he did go there, but I'm sure he'll call when he gets back."

Not a false promise, she was relatively sure. There were things about Sean that didn't suit her lifestyle, but he was a good guy and she didn't picture him deserting Corey.

Of course, she hadn't expected Brad to have ignored his son, seeing him only when it was convenient, or when she made him feel guilty.

Corey shrugged. "Yeah, he was probably missing his sister and nieces."

"His sister? In Hawaii?"

He nodded. "She's a captain."

"In the military?"

Corey shrugged. "What else did he tell you about Hawaii and his sister, honey?"

"That's all." He thought for a moment. "He said he likes to swim in Hawaii. His other sister lives in California but the water isn't as nice there. They all go hiking in the mountains when he visits them."

"When did he tell you all this?"

Corey scrunched up his face. "One time when we went fishing without you."

Alana's thoughts went back to the photographs in Sean's living room. The ones taken of Sean sunning on tropical islands, or skiing in the mountains, or hamming it up in what looked like European cities. In many of them he'd been with kids of various ages.

Distracted by her thoughts, she automatically locked the medicine cabinet, checked to make sure Cindy had locked the cash drawer, and then took Corey's hand.

As they walked to the house, she asked, "Do you know how many brothers and sisters Sean has?"

"Three, I think. No, four."

She knew of one sister for sure. Sean had talked about her once. "Are they all in the military?"

"Huh?"

She smiled. He seemed to be growing up so fast, sometimes she forgot he was only six years old. "Like the army or navy…remember Grandpa's picture in his soldier uniform?"

Corey nodded. "Sean has a picture of the captain in his uniform."

"Captain?"

"Sean's daddy," he said impatiently. "I'm hungry."

"Ah, that captain." Alana grinned. Had Sean told her his father was a captain? Probably he had that first night over dinner. God, that seemed so long ago. "How about just grilled cheese tonight? Butter-pecan ice cream for dessert. Is that okay?"

He nodded happily, and then his eyes lit up. "Hey, I know. Let's call Sean and see if he's home. He can come to dinner. He *loves* butter-pecan ice cream."

"If he is home he's busy, honey." She ushered him through the kitchen door and steered him toward the sink. "That's why he hasn't called. Wash your hands so you can help me butter the bread."

"So what if he's busy? He's gotta eat." He gave her a reproving look. "You always say that when I tell you I'm too busy."

She sighed. "We aren't going to call him now. Maybe tomorrow."

Corey stuck his lower lip out as he stepped up on the stool to wash his hands. He knew better than to argue when she used that tone of voice, but he made it perfectly clear he didn't like her decision. He'd probably give her the silent treatment for a while, which was just as well. Her head was a mess with contradictory thoughts.

Sean had told her he was family-oriented and wanted to settle down, and that was the major reason he and Brenda had cooled their relationship. Alana hadn't believed him. Instead, she'd chosen to think the worst.

And then she'd practically accused him of being footloose without anything but photographs to support her beliefs, photos that really showed how important family was to him. If she hadn't been so busy looking for excuses not to love him, she'd have seen the truth.

Not only was Sean everything she wanted in a friend, he was everything she wanted in a husband. And she'd been ugly and condescending and a coward.

God, why hadn't he defended himself? Reminded her the vacation pictures were of his family. That if he wanted to see them he had to travel. It had nothing to do with him having a restless nature and being unable to stay in one place for long.

"If you don't wanna call him, then can I?" Corey asked, his eyes fretful.

"He'd know I gave you the number."

"So?"

Alana laughed at herself. Corey wasn't a player in the game. He didn't care who called first.

The thought sobered her. How childish could she be? How ironic. Here she'd thought he was too young for her.

What would it hurt to call him? Her pride? That was the least of her worries.

"Well, can I?"

She looked at Corey. He'd been so happy with Sean around. So had she. She sighed. Maybe she should just leave well enough alone. Corey would get over this eventually.

But damn, it wasn't just about Corey.

She marched across the kitchen and picked up the phone before she lost her nerve.

"Yay!" Corey skipped up behind her. "You're calling him." Her heart pounded harder with each number she punched in. She smiled at Corey as she listened to the first and second ring. By the fourth ring, her palms got sticky.

And then the answering machine came on and Sean's voice asked her to leave a message. She opened her mouth. Nothing came out.

The doorbell rang.

Corey ran out of the kitchen.

"Corey, don't open it. Wait for me." She slammed the receiver down when she realized the machine had picked up her voice.

"Damn it." She ran after her son and stopped short when she saw Sean standing outside the door.

"Where have you been?" Corey asked him, one hand on the open door, the other on his hip. "You missed football this week."

"Yeah, sorry," Sean gave him a brief smile, then looked at Alana. "I had a lot to do."

She moistened her lips, trying to think of something to say.

"That's okay," Corey whispered. "Mom's been in a bad mood, anyway."

Sean grinned, his gaze still on her.

She took a deep breath. "He's right. Crow." She faked a shudder. "What a horrible taste."

Comprehension gleamed in Sean's eyes and he stepped inside. "A little salt and pepper should help."

Corey made a face. "What are you guys talking about?"

Alana broke eye contact to look at Corey. "Honey, would you do me a favour? Go check and make sure the dogs have clean water."

He stomped a foot. "But Sean just got here."

"That's okay, sport." Sean cast him a brief glance, and then met Alana's eyes again. "I'm not going anywhere."

"Promise?"

"I promise," he said, his eyes still fastened to hers as Corey trotted off.

"I was just trying to call you," she said as soon as Corey had disappeared.

"Oh? What were you going to tell me?"

She took a deep breath. "That I've missed you."

A smile warmed his eyes. "Anything else?"

She nodded. If he made her get down on all fours, she probably deserved it. "I was wrong."

He didn't say anything. Just waited.

"I was wrong about you not being ready for a family. I was wrong not to give us a chance." She swallowed hard. The lump in her throat wouldn't budge. "But if you're still mad or not interested—"

He crossed the room in three long strides and slid his arms around her, lifting her off the floor. "I love you, Dr. Fletcher. You're not getting rid of me that easily. Besides, I made a promise to your son."

She laughed. "Put me down. I'm not ready for another trip to the hospital."

"Hey, I'm strong." He lowered her to the floor.

"You are," she agreed solemnly. "And smart and funny and loyal, and I very much want to give us another try."

"Honey, you've got me for the long haul," he said, and kissed her.

EPILOGUE

"CAN I SLEEP OVER AT Ritchie's house tonight?"

"Sure," Sean said at the same time Alana said, "Of course you can." They looked at each other and tried not to laugh.

"Cool." Corey hopped off the counter where he'd been talking on the phone and ran to his room.

"Hope we didn't sound too eager."

Chuckling, Sean came up behind her, slid his arms around her waist and cradled her against him. "If we did, he sure didn't notice."

She leaned into him, smiling, happier than she could imagine. "Gosh, a whole night alone. I hope we won't be bored."

"Hmm, I wonder…" He slid his hands up to cup her breasts.

"Hey, stop that."

"Why?"

She giggled. "Corey might catch us."

"News flash. We're married."

"Still, he shouldn't see—ooh." She closed her eyes at the delicious sensation his lips created at the side of her neck.

"Did you say something?"

She felt his smile against her skin and her lips curved, too. "Don't be smug."

"That's not what you said last night," he whispered, and turned her to face him.

They'd only been married seven months, yet it was amazing how well he knew her. How great an effort he'd made to get to know all about her. Corey adored him. Her son had changed before her eyes. He was happy and animated all the time. And Sean's constant encouragement had created a confidence in Corey that thrilled her maternal heart.

How could she have ever had a single doubt about this man?

Cupping her face with his hands, his eyes sparkling wickedly, he whispered, "Come on, let's go get naked."

"Think you can wait until Corey is at Ritchie's?"

"No."

She laughed and gave him a brief kiss. "Have I told you lately how much I love you?"

He smiled. "If it's half as much as I love you, I'll die a happy man."

FORRESTER SQUARE,
*a new Harlequin series,
continues in July 2004 with
ESCAPE THE NIGHT
by Joanne Wayne...*

*Alexandra Webber should never have
returned to Seattle—or fallen in love with
Ben Jessup. Ben and his son live at her
childhood address in Forrester Square,
and for Alexandra, it's like stepping back
in time. Long haunted by recurring
nightmares about the fire that claimed
her parents' lives, she's remembering
things that dangerous people would
rather stay forgotten. But when Alex is
kidnapped, Ben will stop at nothing
to end the nightmare...*

Here's a preview!

CHAPTER ONE

"I CAN'T HELP YOU, BEN. I won't be staying in Seattle much longer." Alexandra stood and walked to the kitchen. "We should eat, and then you should leave."

The mood between them became even more strained. He'd upset her, and Ben wasn't even sure why. Before yesterday, he'd thought of Alexandra only as an attractive, independent young woman with a barbed tongue and a lousy disposition.

But she was a lot more complex than that. And in spite of her problems, he was still convinced she'd be perfect to run a child-care center at Seattle Memorial.

Not that it mattered. She'd made up her mind, and he was smart enough to know when he'd hit a brick wall.

ALEXANDRA STOOD AT THE large windows, her favorite part of her loft apartment, and stared at the night sky. She was so very, very tired, but sleep would only bring nightmares. The fire. The smoke. The screams.

She went to the kitchen, poured the last of the wine into a clean flute, and took it back to her chair beside the window, the one Ben had sat in when he'd talked of his wife.

Alexandra had to admit that the story had gotten to

her. Ben had obviously loved Doug's mother very
much and desperately wanted to keep his promise to
her. His mistake had been in thinking Alexandra could
help him with his project. But he didn't know—and
she had no intention of telling him—that the ghosts
that lived in her memory were becoming more real
than the people who inhabited her world.

If she didn't leave Seattle soon, she'd go completely
crazy. Unless…unless Gary Devlin did turn out to be
her father. Then she'd do whatever was best for him.

She leaned back in the chair and closed her eyes.
Exhausted, she let her mind drift back into the tunnels
as sleep overtook her. She was running, chasing a man
who was always a step ahead of her. Her lungs burned
and her legs ached, but no matter how she tried, she
couldn't catch up with him. Finally, she fell against a
support post, gasping for breath.

Only it wasn't a post. It was a man. She jerked her
head up and stared into the face of Dr. Ben Jessup.
She woke up, her pulse racing. It was the horrible
nightmare that usually haunted her sleep, but still she
was shaking.

She wished he'd never come over tonight, never
talked to her about his dead wife and about the promise he'd made. It wasn't fair for him to pull her into
his problems when she had so many of her own.

It wasn't right for him to need her.

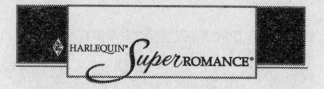

HARLEQUIN® *Super*ROMANCE®

...there's more to the story!

Superromance.
A *big* satisfying read about unforgettable
characters. Each month we offer *six* very different
stories that range from family drama to adventure
and mystery, from highly emotional stories to
romantic comedies—and much more! Stories
about people you'll believe in and care about.
Stories too compelling to put down....

Our authors are among today's *best* romance
writers. You'll find familiar names and talented
newcomers. Many of them are award winners—
and you'll see why!

If you want the biggest and best
in romance fiction, you'll get it
from Superromance!

Emotional, Exciting, Unexpected...

HARLEQUIN®
*M*akes any time special ®

Visit us at www.eHarlequin.com

HSDIR1

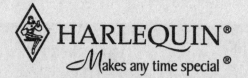